MACKINAC PASSAGE:
THE BOATHOUSE
MYSTERY

MACKINAC PASSAGE: THE BOATHOUSE MYSTERY

Robert A. Lytle
Illustrated by Karen Howell

Thunder Bay Press

Holt, Michigan

Published by Thunder Bay Press
Designed and typeset by Maureen MacLaughlin-Morris
Maps by Karen Howell and Advancing Imaging
Printed by Eerdmans Printing Company, Grand Rapids,
        Michigan
Cover painting by Karen Howell

ISBN: 1-882376-29-3

Printed in the United States of America

97 98 99 2000   2 3 4 5 6 7 8 9

Holt, Michigan

Acknowledgements

This second *Mackinac Passage* story is completed with a host of helpers whose contributions, small and large, have made its making as enjoyable as it has been entertaining: To my family who have put up with my absence, either physically or mentally, from the home scene. To my co-workers who have tolerated my bouts of furious non-productivity at the store. To Dave Boothe, Julie and Ken Barnes, and Diane Davis' for their fishing expertise which aided in the early chapters. To Ray Lawson and Ken Johnson who again proofread and critiqued early drafts pointing out subtle omissions in plot as well as glaring grammatical errors throughout. And once again to my Les Cheneaux friends whose intrusion into their lives I beg forgiveness. I owe you all a lifelong debt of gratitude.

Dedication:

This book is dedicated to those whose good fortune it is to have experienced life in the Les Cheneaux Islands.

*Pierre slid to the bottom of the
canoe and dreamed of better days.*

CHAPTER 1
RESCUE

Monday, June 30, 1952, 2:00 p.m.

This summer, she is not going so good, Pierre
LeSoeur thought as he carried his fishing pole from
his shack. *I have no beaver to sell at the Sault. Without pelts, I have to find work for the winter. My father was right. The flattail, she is gone. All my traps
catch is the little muskrat, worth nothing except to
eat.*

The aging fur trapper stepped into the canoe and
set the fishing pole next to his double-barreled shotgun. Pushing away from the marshy bank into Bass
Cove Lake, Pierre hooked a bait perch through the back
and set it into the water. The small fish took twenty
feet of line and swam nearby just under the surface of
the deep, island pond. Pierre attached his balsa bobber
and let out another thirty feet of line. Today, he would
catch the monstrous pike that had gotten away so many
times. He set the pole between his legs and lay back in
the warm, summer afternoon to consider his plight.

1

That evening he would check his traps, but he knew what he would find—nothing, save a muskrat or two. He was out of money, and had been for a month. If he was going to eat anything but fish and muskrat, he'd have to steal from the boathouses where the wealthy resorters often left food, beer, and soft drinks. Sometimes he'd even find loose change lying about which he'd spend at the bar in town. As long as he did no damage to the boathouses, none of the rich cottagers ever noticed the loss.

Life in the north is not like it was, Pierre sighed. For two centuries, the LeSoeur men had lived well on the beaver trade. Pierre's father had told him that he would have to learn something new, but Pierre would not listen. He had tried once as a boy to work in the lumber camps, but it was not for him. He went back to trapping and held onto the old ways becoming poorer every year.

A warm, offshore breeze rocked the canoe moving it slowly across the lake. The bobber bounced occasionally as the bait fish swam below. Pierre slid to the bottom of the canoe and leaned his head against the seat. He dozed in the warm sun and dreamed of better days.

A monumental blast in the distance startled Pierre out of a deep, mid-afternoon nap. He lurched forward, his small craft tipping dangerously from side to side.

"Sacre bleu!" he yelled opening his eyes. *Is that thunder I hear?* he thought. *Where is the storm? There is not a cloud in the sky. It must be a dream.* He looked over the side and watched his bobber slash across the surface. The little bait perch also felt the distant concussion. A tremendous echo reverberated throughout the Snows. *It is no dream. Something has exploded.*

Pierre glanced in all directions. His gaze fell upon a thick billow of black smoke emerging over the tree-tops a half-mile away to the west. *A boat, she has blown up. I must hurry to the wreck and salvage what I can.*

He reeled in his line, released the perch, and paddled to the shore closest to the big lake. He hopped out and dragged the canoe over the five-foot isthmus that separated Bass Cove Lake on LaSalle Island from the immense waters of Lake Huron. He pushed off from the pebbly beach and jumped into his canoe. Pierre plied the water with strong, rhythmic strokes guiding him in the precise direction of the black cloud.

It must have happened near the mouth of the little passage, he thought. The southern tip of LaSalle Island still blocked his view of the wreckage. He rounded the point and saw, just ahead, a small, white-hulled outboard. It was loaded to its gunwales with passengers and moved into Bosely Channel past the smoking hulk of a large speedboat. Pierre sensed that those aboard were the survivors of the wreck and may have lost something of value in the accident.

He paddled up to the sunken vessel and began his search. In the clear, shallow water, Pierre found the brass casing of a spent 30-06 rifle shell. Nearby, he spotted pieces of a shattered windshield and the twisted remains of a rifle. He made larger circles around the Bosely Channel entrance. After an hour of futile inspection, he pulled his canoe onto the bank of LaSalle Island closest to the smoking vessel. There he would explore the land hoping to find something on shore.

As he wallowed through the soft sand, he heard a thrashing sound a few feet inland behind the wall of reeds. It sounded like a wounded beaver.

I have no traps here, he thought. *What could it be?*

He pulled his canoe through the dense reeds onto the shore and found a huge man lying on his back, perhaps at death's door. He wore blue pants, white shirt, and a blue jacket with emblems on the shoulders. *He is police!* Pierre stepped back, ready to run. No, the man had no badge. Pierre looked closer at the shoulder patch. "Dockmaster—Mackinac Island," it read. Pierre wasn't sure what that was; but if he was a <u>master,</u> he must be important. Perhaps he was rich, as well. The man's dark blue pants were torn. He was scratched and bleeding. He began to groan. His eyes were squinted as Pierre rolled him on his side. Pierre remembered his purpose in coming and reached into the man's hip pocket. There he found a thick billfold. Pierre smiled when he saw its contents, a stack of twenty dollar bills.

The large man blinked, slowly gaining consciousness. Pierre slipped the wallet into his jacket and stepped back. Was it possible that the injured man was not dying but only stunned from the explosion? Pierre pondered the situation. Perhaps this wealthy man had been blown far away from his companions. He may have been left for dead when they couldn't find him. *I will be rewarded generously for saving his life,* Pierre reasoned.

The large man began to stir. "What happened?" Fats moaned, shaking his head. "Where am I? Who are you?" He blinked at the oddly dressed man holding a shotgun before him.

4

"You ask many questions, monsieur," Pierre said with a smile. "You appear to have nothing broken except your boat, n'est-ce pas?" He waved the barrel of his shotgun toward the remains of the black-hulled speedboat.

"My boat!" Fats blurted out. He paused. "What about those brats?" he snarled. "I can't let them get away."

"It is too late for that, monsieur," Pierre replied, surprised at the rich man's belligerent nature. "A small bateau was disappearing down the little channel maybe an hour ago as I arrived. There were many aboard, but she was moving faster as I approached. They are perhaps many miles away by now."

"Then you've got to hide me. Take me to where you live, now! The cops'll be here any minute."

Pierre stood over Fats, slowly reassessing the situation. *This is a dilemma*, Pierre deliberated. *The injured man is, perhaps, not a respectable person. But then,* he shrugged, *neither am I.* Finally, Pierre shook his head. "No, I cannot take you to my place, monsieur," he replied. "If the police find you in my care, I will be arrested as your confederate. I sense your crime is very serious. No, monsieur, I cannot risk that. As a gentleman of the north, I will help you find shelter. Beyond that, you must fend for yourself."

Pierre pushed the canoe into the channel and held it as Fats managed to load himself aboard. Pierre then slipped into the stern, holding the shotgun in his lap. He paddled along Bosely Channel, searching for a suitable place to discharge his unwanted passenger.

Pierre approached the large, three-stall boathouse at the end of the channel. He had broken into it and stolen food the night before. He couldn't leave him there. Only an unoccupied cottage or an abandoned boathouse would do. He paddled out of Bosely Channel and through Urie Bay. Once around Urie Point, he saw a small island with a cabin. An old man had lived there whom he hadn't seen for two summers. That would be perfect. He would leave the man there.

As they approached the island, Fats saw a fast-moving boat coming from Cedarville.

"Hide!" Fats yelled.

Pierre plunged the canoe through a wall of tall reeds and watched a Mackinac County Police boat with two uniformed men aboard race toward Bosely Channel. The craft flew past them into Urie Bay.

Fats watched as it disappeared and then turned his attention to the small cabin ahead. He immediately recognized it as Harold Geetings' island where Harold and he had made counterfeit money for the past two years and transported it at night to Mackinac Island. "You can't leave me here," he said, "The cops will search Harold's place next."

"Oui, monsieur," Pierre said in exasperation. He turned and looked along the LaSalle Island shoreline. At the end of a row of small docks and boathouses stood a structure ravaged by years of neglect. "Voila. Your new home is just ahead," he said pointing to the decrepit boathouse. "No one will look for you here. It is ideal, non?"

"No! This is worse!" Fats screamed in panic. "It's falling down. There's no dock to it. I could never get off. Besides, how can I get inside? The boat door is closed. The water's too deep. I can't swim."

Pierre grew angry. He raised his gun pointing it toward the ample target in front of him. He shook his head, "My canoe, she will not slip under the gate. You must grab the door and force it high enough to duck inside. You will get out and provide for yourself."

"You're going to leave me in an abandoned boat-house with no way to get to shore?"

"Non, monsieur. There is a sturdy canoe inside. It has been above the water line for many years. You may use it to travel wherever you wish. Besides, you have no choice. You do as I say or I pull the trigger."

"Why, you miserable . . . "

"Move ahead, monsieur. The darkness will be coming soon and you will not be able to see inside. I suggest you waste no more time. Au revoir, monsieur."

Pierre nudged the gun barrel into Fats' ribs and then paddled the canoe up to the door of the weather-beaten boathouse. Fats leaned forward, braced one foot outside on the stone crib, and strained to lift the overhanging gate. The canoe's bow dipped. The left side of the door screeched and moved just high enough to allow Fats' head to slip under into the darkened building. Fats peered in and found a mass of cobwebs.

"Climb inside now, monsieur," Pierre ordered.

"I'll get you for this," Fats growled as he lifted his bulk into the old building. He pulled himself onto the inside deck and kicked hard at the canoe trying to overturn it.

Pierre backpaddled quickly and the bow bobbed free of the lopsided door. He turned and started back to his cabin. In the distance he heard the police boat returning from its search of Bosely Channel. Pierre slipped his canoe into the tall reeds near the tiny island. The police boat coasted into the clearing thirty feet ahead. Pierre watched two uniformed men step onto Harold

7

Geetings' dock. They entered the cabin and came out minutes later carrying a printing press and two heavy boxes. Pierre watched as they boarded up the windows and bolted the cabin door before placing the items in their boat. They stepped into the launch, started the engine, and headed toward Cedarville.

As Pierre waited in the weeds, he made a change of plans. *I will not check my traps tonight,* he thought as he opened the fat man's wallet. *This will be a night of celebration.* He counted out three brand new twenties, not noticing their identical serial numbers, and stuffed them in a shirt pocket. He folded the rest and slid them into a seam of his jacket.

I will go into town and visit my friends at the Cedar Bar, Pierre smiled. *They will think differently of this old, French trapper. They will treat me with respect,* he thought, patting the wad in his pocket. *Tonight, they will be begging ME for drinks.*

Pierre paddled toward Cedarville. He had no idea how near he was to the place his new-found wealth had so recently been printed.

The Bon Air was hopping ...

CHAPTER 2
MEANWHILE, IN TOWN ...

Monday, June 30 3:30 p.m.

It was a hot, windless afternoon. Six ceiling fans spun silently over the noisy soda shop patrons who were mostly resort teenagers and their little brothers and sisters. The Wurlitzer jukebox in the corner was cranking out "Rag Mop," but it could barely penetrate the clamor of the four, blue Hamilton-Beach blenders whipping up malts and milk shakes behind the counter. Kids shuffled from one table to the next waiting for a chair, while those seated seemed in no rush to leave. Some slurped their straws at the bottoms of heavy soda glasses while others scooped the dregs of Jersey Muds and Brown Cows with their long, stainless steel spoons.

It seemed, at any given moment, that half of the people in the Bon Air had something enormously clever to say to which the other half responded in uproarious laughter. The Bon Air was hopping but no more so than on any other summers' day for the past fifty years.

If any of the Les Cheneaux Islands' resorters under the age of eighteen had any concern about the ninety-

9

degree heat, they had not come to the Bon Air to complain about it. Mrs. Clark stood at the cash register ringing sales as fast as possible. Now that she couldn't rely on her soda jerk, Jack Frazier, to tell a real dollar bill from a fake one, she had to do all the cash transactions herself. She glanced up from her customer just as the front screen door opened.

She stared as an entourage of two Michigan State troopers, seven adults, and five teenagers quietly entered the Bon Air. In moments, all the chattering and laughing stopped; everyone's attention turned to the new arrivals. Even the jukebox paused between records, seemingly awaiting an explanation. The Bon Air had never experienced a moment of such quiet anticipation.

Dr. Hinken led the parade and motioned to Mrs. Clark for a word. She nodded and escorted the unusual party to the back room, which was used almost exclusively by the Les Cheneaux Rotary Club for its Tuesday luncheon meetings. When the door closed, a murmur of excitement crept around the tables. The selection arm of the jukebox placed a Johnny Raye record on the turntable. The speakers blasted "Cry" into the silent crowd, rekindling the previous raucous commotion.

"What are two state policemen doing with Eddie, Dan, and Kate?" murmured some of the kids.

"They're always up to something," others replied, "but never anything that would get them into any real trouble. Besides, if they had done something really bad, why would they be here at the Bon Air?"

"Yes, and what's that other kid and his older sister doing with them? And the hermit from Elliot Bay? And all those parents? Why was everyone so serious?"

10

Grim regard was not a common expression worn on the faces of Les Cheneaux resorters. Quite the contrary, for this was the exclusive retreat that wealthy Cincinnati and Chicago families had been keeping secret from the rest of the world since the late 1800s. Every June for over fifty years they journeyed north by train and boat to enjoy the cool Straits of Mackinac breezes and the crisp, northern Michigan air. They relaxed in their lavish summer homes. They swept through the Les Cheneaux channels and bays in their sleek mahogany speedboats and tall, graceful sailboats. No, the solemn demeanor of the arrivals who were making their way to the back of the Bon Air was, indeed, an odd occurrence.

With the door to the small, private room closed, Mrs. Clark took her pencil and pad from her white apron and moved around the circular table. Dr. Daniel Hinken and his wife, Ann, ordered cherry sodas. Mr. and Mrs. Terkel requested strawberry sundaes. Pete's parents, Howard and Averill Jenkins, ordered Cokes. The two uniformed troopers asked for coffee—black, no sugar. The four fifteen-year-olds, the twins, Kate and Dan Hinken, Eddie Terkel, and Pete Jenkins, asked for Jersey Muds. Pete's older sister, Cara, opted for a Brown Cow. The last person to order was the old man, Harold Geetings, who sat quietly still in handcuffs.

Harold looked up and smiled, perhaps for the first time in two years. "I'd like a Jersey Mud, too," he said. "I haven't had one in ages, and it looks as if it may be my last for a while. I'm glad this is over," he said, sinking back into his wooden chair. "Today, a burden has been lifted from my shoulders, one that has made the last two years the worst of my life. In hindsight, I realize the thirty years before that have been one sad mistake after another. Somehow, I had convinced myself that, in order to earn people's respect, I had to become a published author. Until I did, I rejected their companionship and buried myself in my cabin. I can never recover all of those lost years," he said, glancing around the table. "I can only hope you'll accept me if I ever return from prison."

Mrs. Clark carried the orders out of the small room to the soda fountain. As she opened the door, two more uniformed men entered. The four officers immediately huddled around a map of the Les Cheneaux Islands. They asked Dr. Hinken for directions to Bosely Channel where the mystery speedboat had exploded. Next, they inquired about Harold Geetings' cabin where the counterfeit money had been printed. Finally, they asked for the way to the red, double boathouse where the *Griffin* was moored.

Two of the officers left with the map as Mrs. Clark returned with the fountain orders. The taller of the two remaining state troopers leaned back and took a legal pad from his briefcase. The other began the interrogation, asking first for Mr. Geetings' account of the past two summers.

Everyone else sat spellbound as the old man related the events that finally brought him here to the Bon Air this day. They quickly realized that nothing had escaped the watchful eye of the reclusive writer. He had been a witness to all the sailing regattas, Les Cheneaux Club excursions, and the Les Cheneaux Yacht Club parties. He'd watched the Elliot, Islington, and Cedar Inn Hotel activities; he'd monitored the romances and courtships of all the summer resorters.

Somehow, with virtually no direct contact, he had written complete novels and dozens of short stories about all the people of the Les Cheneaux Islands for the last four decades.

Only three resorters, Dr. and Mrs. Hinken and Pete's mom, Averill Jenkins, knew he had even aspired to be a writer. To the rest of the Les Cheneaux cottagers, Harold Geetings was nothing more than a cantankerous old man who's only wish was to remain in the solitude of his tiny island in Elliot Bay, a request most were happy to accommodate.

He had gradually spent all of his considerable inheritance on writing materials, food, and fuel. Two summers ago, he had finally run out of funds. In desperation, he had taken up with Gerald FitzRoberts, a Mackinac Island summer employee. Harold was forced to become an unwilling partner in a large, underworld counterfeiting scheme. He and Fats, as his accomplice was called, printed the phony currency on Harold's island in Elliot Bay. They transported it at night to Mackinac Island, where they passed it off at their bike rental station, the front for the illegal operation. It wasn't until that very morning that Harold realized that Pete and his friends had discovered the scam. The youths evidently had suspected Mr. Geetings for some time and followed him to Mackinac Island. There, they watched Fats bash in the brains of a third member of the gang, Joey Cahill, who had carelessly blown their cover. The four terrified teens fled the murder scene in panic and were able to escape from Mackinac Island during the night on their small sailboat, the *Griffin*.

The next day, when Harold and Fats discovered who had witnessed Joey's murder, they pursued them in their speedboat. They were zeroing in on the teenagers near BoselyChannel that afternoon, with Fats aiming his rifle and Harold steering the boat. The old man looked up from the wheel and realized that the youths Fats was about to kill were the sons and daughters of the resort people about whom he'd written so many stories.

There was Averill's son driving the boat. Averill's daughter was scrunched on the floor with the Hinken and Terkel's children. Harold suddenly knew he couldn't let Fats kill them, even if it meant spending the rest of his life in prison. He jerked back on the throttle and turned the wheel to make Fats lose his balance. It almost worked, too, but Fats regained his footing and came after Harold with his gun. The next thing Harold knew, he was lying on the living room floor in the Hinken's summer home. Dr. Hinken was waving smelling salts in front of his nose. Thank goodness the youngsters were safe, but he still didn't know what had happened to Fats.

The trooper with the note pad was scribbling furiously while the other continued asking questions.

Finally, the older officer leaned back in his chair. "Is there anything else you'd like to add, Mr. Geetings?" he asked.

"Just one request," Harold said softly. "If Averill would be willing, I'd be forever grateful if she could store my papers until I return. I hold little hope now that they'll ever be published, but they still mean a great deal to me."

"Oh, Harold," Averill Jenkins said, "you poor, dear man. You have no idea how many times the Elliot Row people have worried about you being alone on your tiny island. You refused our help so often we had no choice but to leave you to yourself. Still, we always held hope that something would change and you would rejoin our circle of friends." Then she turned to the policemen, "If there's anything we can do for his defense, please let us know."

The troopers next turned to Dan and asked him for his account of the past several weeks.

After Dan, each of the other teenagers made their reports. An hour later, as Cara was finishing her part of the story, the screen door to the Bon Air swung open. The two troopers who had left in search of Fats walked in and made their way to the back room.

"There's no sign of Mr. FitzRoberts anywhere," the first one said. "We found the wreckage of a large speedboat at the end of Bosely Channel. When it ran aground it must have exploded and blown him back into Lake Huron. There's a strong undertow that undoubtedly carried his body out into the lake. As cold as the water is, he may never come up. One thing's for sure, he didn't survive the blast. There are parts of the boat strewn over a quarter mile in all directions of the channel."

"Well," Dr. Hinken said standing, "I think it's time we returned to our cottages. Perhaps we'll all be more mindful of the dangers that can come even in our private little corner of paradise."

At that, the four policemen escorted Harold Geetings through the crowded front room and out of the Bon Air to the squad car. The rest of the party followed and returned to the city dock. They boarded the *Polly Ann,* and Dr. Hinken headed her out of Cedarville Bay toward Big LaSalle Island.

15

"Pete will tell you all about it at the pump tonite."

CHAPTER 3
THE COMMUNITY PUMP

Monday, June 30 6:00 p.m.

The Hinken's long, white-hulled Hacker-Craft cruised gracefully along Cedarville Channel past Cincinnati Row and into Elliot Bay. Dr. Hinken adjusted the throttle bringing her alongside the Elliot Hotel visitors' dock. Eddie and Dan jumped onto the wide, wooden pier, each taking a line and tying it to a piling. Then they helped Mr. and Mrs. Jenkins ashore, with Pete and Cara helping themselves.

"See you tomorrow, Pete," Eddie said as Pete stepped onto the dock.

"Come to our place after noon," Kate added. "We've got to plan our boathouse potluck for this Wednesday. It's Dan's and my turn to host it, and we'd like you to be our guest."

"Sure," Pete replied, fending the *Polly Ann* away from the dock with his foot. "But I'll have to check it first with my parents." He waved to his friends as Dr. Hinken reversed the boat away from the pier.

16

As the four Jenkins turned toward shore, Pete's sister, Cara, hissed at her younger brother, "You'll have to check it with your parents before you so much as sneeze, from now on. How could you have gone off to Mackinac Island making Mom and Dad think that all you were doing was visiting Dan and Kate's relatives? Honestly, Pete, sometimes it worries me to think we're related."

"I tried to tell you about Mr. Geetings and the counterfeit money, but you wouldn't listen," Pete argued.

"You might try to be a little more convincing next time," Howard Jenkins admonished.

"I'm sorry," Pete moaned. "A few hours ago, I'd have given anything to have changed all that."

"Well," Mrs. Jenkins said, her hand on Pete's shoulder, "At least I hope you've learned a lesson. I'm sure you'll fill us in on all your plans in the future."

The four Jenkins walked past several elegantly attired hotel guests at the head of the dock.

"I promise," Pete said. "We were just having fun. None of us thought we'd get so mixed up in any real danger that we couldn't at least get help."

"Maybe so," Cara added, "but just don't forget how easy it was going from having fun to just plain being had."

"Yeah, it sure happened fast," Pete admitted.

When the Jenkins turned to follow the path to their cabin, they were met by several of the Elliot Row cottagers.

"What's going on, Howard?" asked Russell Patrick. His place was three doors down from the Jenkins. "Why all the policemen?"

"It's a long story, Russell," Howard replied. "Pete will tell you all about it at the pump tonight."

"We'll be there," Frances Wirtle said, standing next to Mr. Patrick. "We wouldn't miss this for anything."

————

That night after dinner, Pete and his dad each carried two empty water pails along the dusty trail to the well. Soon Pete was describing the whole story to his Elliot Row neighbors as they sat around the pump. Everyone from Mr. and Mrs. Flowers, whose cabin was next to the hotel, to Doc and Mary Davis, whose place was at the far end of Elliot Row, brought their pails and squeezed onto the rickety platform overlooking Elliot Bay. They listened as Pete described Harold Geetings' disappointments as a writer and the financial hardship that led him to his involvement with the East Coast gangsters. Pete explained how he and his Cincinnati Row friends had discovered the counterfeiting scheme, sailed to Mackinac Island, witnessed a murder, and then out-raced Fats and Harold's speedboat back to Bosely Channel.

7:00 p.m. Long's Old Boathouse, Elliot Bay

In the fading light of day Fats thrashed wildly at the cobwebs. They were everywhere. Exhausted from his long day and the wounds suffered from his boat accident, he stretched out on the decaying dock and slipped into a restless sleep.

10:15 p.m. The Elliot Row Water Pump

The sky in the west was crystal clear as the sun approached the horizon. A few stringy clouds blazed overhead with an amazing splendor of gold, orange, crimson, and purple. As Pete finished telling his remarkable tale, faint stars began to glow. Soon, more celestial lights blossomed and filled the heavens. An umbrella of soft radiance shone down on Pete and his rapt Elliot Row listeners.

An entire battalion of mosquitoes gathered nearby delighted that so many warm-blooded guests had joined them for dinner. Bats began to dart through the trees, feasting on the mosquitoes.

"I guess we'd better get home before the bears join us, too," Pete's dad suggested.

The cottagers picked up their pails and returned to their dimly lit, Elliot Row cabins. Pete followed his dad, the trail clearly visible with only the starlight to guide them. A shimmering curtain of Northern Lights slowly cascaded across the sky. Cedar trees cast in silver silhouette stood beside the path in silky silence. Fireflies flitted by, featuring their own flickering phosphorescence.

The front screen door slapped softly against its wooden frame. Pete crossed the living room and set his pails on the kitchen stand. His mom had left a lamp burning in the living room window before she and Cara had closed their books and gone to bed.

"How about joining me for the Sunrise Service, Pete?" his father whispered. That was Howard Jenkins' term for early morning fishing.

"Sure, Dad," Pete whispered. "But right now, I think I'll go down to the dock for awhile. I'm still kind of wired from everything that's happened today." He checked the glowing hands of the wind-up clock on the lamp table. It was 10:30. He should be exhausted, but he wasn't.

"Okay, but don't stay up too late. Tomorrow comes early and the big ones are expecting us. I'd hate to disappoint them."

Pete made his way down the steep, stone walkway to the shore and out to the end of the narrow dock. The air was warm and calm. He sat on the last plank between the *Flossy* and the *Tiny Tin*, the Jenkins' two small outboards. As he dangled his feet in the cool water a thousand sounds surrounded him: fish rose and slapped in the bay feeding on a hatch of mayflies; bats screeched overhead; frogs croaked along the shore, and crickets cricked in the woods nearby. The night was anything but still. The last two days had passed so quickly. So much had happened. He needed time to think, to be by himself.

10:35 p.m. Long's Old Boathouse

Fats awoke from a terrifying nightmare. In the dream, dozens of snakes and huge spiders were holding him down in a cave while thousands of bats slashed at his face flying about him in chaotic frenzy. He sat up with a start. His eyes darted in blind confusion. Sweat poured from his face. It was several moments before he focused on the darkened boathouse beams high overhead. What he saw drove shivers deep into his soul. Suspended from the rafters were thousands of bats. Startled by the movements of the man below, the largest ones dropped from their roosts eager to protect their young from the intruder. In moments, the rickety building was alive with chirps and squeaks and wildly flapping wings. Fats fell to his hands and knees. He clenched his arms over his head and convulsed in horrified gales of dread. Bats whipped about him grazing his head and back. A few escaped under the lopsided boathouse door into the starlit evening.

10:35 p.m. The Jenkins' Dock

Pete was startled by an uproar coming from the old green boathouse forty yards away. *What's going on down at bat haven? I've never heard them carry on like this.*

Pete laid back on the dock and stared into the star-filled sky. *How close did I come to being killed this afternoon?* he wondered. *Probably, less than an inch. Fats' bullet was that close. Instead of disintegrating my head, it only blew out the Flossy's windshield.* Pete shook involuntarily. *That's too close for me. I'll never get myself in a pickle like that again.*

Then Pete thought about Kate. When she held his hand that afternoon and told him how he'd saved her life, she looked into his eyes with an emotion he had never seen before. He could still feel her soft, warm lips where she'd kissed his cheek. She was, unquestionably, the most fantastic girl on the planet.

The clamor from the old boathouse continued. The mosquitoes began to home in on Pete's neck and ankles. His dad would be waking him up in a few hours to go fishing. Pete decided he'd better get to bed. It wasn't all that peaceful down at the dock, anyway. He headed for shore and up the stone path.

Pete tiptoed across the porch into the living room and felt his way to his bedroom. He peeled off his jeans, shoes, and socks leaving them next to his bed. He turned back the heavy quilt blankets and slid between the thick, cotton sheets. As great as it was to have met his new Cincinnati Row friends and been able to join in all their social activities, it was still a terrific relief to be home safe in his own bed.

He closed his eyes and sank into the thick, goose feather mattress. Sleep swept over him like a down-bound freighter.

More bats. They were everywhere.

CHAPTER 4
REVENGE

Monday June 30, 10:40 p.m.

Fats awakened again. The stench was overpowering. His body was wracked in intense, cramping pain. He was hungry. He was wet. He was miserably cold. His eyes slowly adjusted to what little moonlight entered the rundown boathouse. He remembered where he was—and why. He recalled the tremendous din of bats flying around him earlier. All was quiet now. His presence must have scared the hideous creatures away.

No, Fats realized, *they're still here. It's just like on Mackinac. Some stay behind while others feed on flying insects throughout the night and then return to their roosts at dawn.* He lay still for a moment, his muscles clenched. He ached everywhere from the explosion. Something cold lay on his bare neck. He reached instinctively toward it and brought his right hand in front of his face. It was dark and soft and smeary. It smelled like . . . it must be . . . bat guano. He felt across his head and shoulders. He was covered with it. He was laying on it. It was everywhere.

He shuddered in disgust. He bumped his shoulder against an object that moved slightly. It thumped a sort of hollow note and a faint rustling came from inside.

23

More bats. He remembered cramming himself against an upside-down canoe as he was being bombarded from every angle by the darting pests.

As miserable as he was, Fats realized that if the canoe was still in one piece, he would be able to move about, at least at night. It would be his means of escape. The abandoned boathouse would provide sufficient shelter where no one would ever look for him. He sensed that the old Frenchman who brought him to the boathouse was no friend of the law and would be unlikely to tell the police about him. Still, it made him nervous that someone knew he was there. He lay in the dark, slowly forming a plan.

He remembered his wallet he had stuffed with counterfeit twenties as he rushed from his room back on Mackinac that morning. At the time, he didn't know why he'd grabbed the fake money, he was only going to be gone for an hour, but now he was glad he did. It would be his ticket out of this mess.

He reached in his hip pocket for his billfold. It wasn't there! He tried his jacket, his shirt, his sleeves. It was gone! In a flash, he remembered lying on the shore after the explosion and through the haze of subconsciousnes, seeing the Frenchman slipping something inside his jacket. That little weasel had stolen his wallet! Now, what would he do?

Fats vowed he would get revenge. Somehow, someway, he would get his chance. He would see to it that it would cost the Frenchman his life.

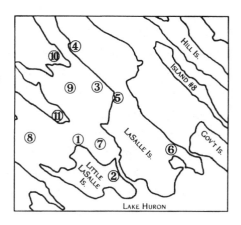

CHAPTER 5
AT ABOUT THE SAME TIME . . .

Monday, June 30. 10:45 p.m.

It was well after sundown as Mickey O'Flynn sat in his old, leaky canoe. His small vessel bobbed among the tall reeds as he stared intently at the red, double boathouse two hundred yards across Cedarville Channel. Holding his bamboo pole, he gazed, not at the bobber, for his line had no hook, but at his next target.

This last month had been horrible for Mickey. He was fired from his job at the quarry when he lost his temper and smashed the foreman in the mouth. That wasn't so bad; he didn't like the job anyway. He was a lumberman. So what was he doing loading limestone onto freighters, anyway? He didn't belong on a dock. He belonged in the forests among the tall pines.

Och, how he longed for the old days, hearing the ring of double-ended axes and the buzz of two-man saws. He yearned for the calls of his mates as they hollered, "Timber!" and then watched as a two hundred-foot pine tree crashed through the woods and thundered

25

to the forest floor. For several moments all would be still as the other lumbermen gazed in awe. Then the axes and saws would start again and Mickey would return to his work.

At night in the bunkhouse the Irish and the French, the Micks and the Frogs, would have at it, fighting about anything and everything. How he loved to bloody the faces of those high and mighty French-Canadians. Mickey was the toughest of the Irishmen and it was his self-appointed duty to take on any new Frog that came to camp. It was a task he relished. He loved working over a Frenchman giving him a scar on his face he would keep for the rest of his life. They were so smug with their high-paying jobs while the Irish worked at the menial tasks in the camp.

But now the great Michigan pineries were gone. Mickey watched the last lumber camp broken up in the spring of '22, thirty years ago, here, right outside of Cedarville. His Irish cronies went off to the factories in Detroit or to work on farms. They found women and become family men while Mickey knocked around the Snows taking odd jobs when he could find them and stealing from gardens and begging for meals when he couldn't. He worked off and on at Port Dolomite as a laborer loading freighters. But Mickey O'Flynn wasn't one to take orders, so he was more often off work than on. Right now he was off. He had no money for rent, so he was turned out of the boarding house to sleep wherever he could find a place to lay his head. Lately, that was a bat-infested boathouse in Elliot Bay. He was living from hand to mouth stealing from the wealthy resorters' boathouses, mainly. He'd worry about winter when it came.

When the last of the lights went out in Cincinnati Row, he set his pole down and paddled swiftly across the two hundred-yard channel directly into the red, double boathouse. He pushed aside a narrow, white-hulled, mahogany speedboat and wedged his canoe against the dock. He scrambled onto the deck and hurried to the refrigerator. He opened its door and the light inside illuminated the contents as well as Mickey's surroundings. On a bench to his right he spied a bright leather change purse.

Mickey O'Flynn hit paydirt. It was fat with coins. He shoved it into his pocket and then turned his attention back to the old, GE refrigerator. He scooped up a loaf of bread, some cheese, a package of sandwich meat, and a couple of Nehi grape sodas. He returned to his canoe and started for the dilapidated boathouse in Elliot Bay where he'd been staying for the past several weeks. Once in the moonlight, however, he opened the small coin holder. He counted out four dollars in quarters and immediately changed his plans.

He spun his canoe around and headed along the mainland shore to the Cedar Bar in town. Along the way he devoured the food, barely breaking his paddling rhythm. He decided he'd have a few beers when he got to the tavern, but mainly he'd go to hear what the other men were saying. Perhaps he'd find a way to steal something worth a lot more than a few coins and some food. When the fishermen got a little liquor in them, their tongues might loosen up a bit. Plus, with the wealthy resorters around, he might find a way to resolve all of his problems.

By midnight, at two bits a beer, Seamus was getting a little loosened up himself. The room was becoming darker as more men rolled in. And louder, too. Resorters, fishermen, and local men were telling their stories and laughing at an ever-increasing pitch. The jukebox was becoming less a source of entertainment as it was a background of discord. Mickey sat at the end of the bar watching Judy, the pretty brunette waitress, becoming lovelier by the minute. She flitted among the tables, giggling at each of her customer's witty remarks. She avoided Mickey's constant stare, however, and stayed as far from him as possible. The only person who'd said anything to Mickey was Sam, the bartender, and all he'd said was, "What'll it be, Paddy?" Mickey hated that old Irish nickname, but he was in no position to get the owner riled. Besides, he wasn't there to talk, especially to Sam. He was there to listen. Maybe he'd move from the bar to a table. *Aye, that's it. If I sit at a table, Judy will have to wait on me. I'll just amble over and join the men in the far corner. They've been inhaling drinks like bilge pumps on a garbage scow. Maybe I'll even get a few free drinks if I play my cards right.*

Mickey stepped, nearly fell actually, from the tall bar stool and worked his way unsteadily through the crowd. He pulled up a chair next to the raucous table. In the darkest corner he recognized the least likely man in all the Snows sitting at the head of the group, each of the men listening to his every word. It was that old, French trapper, Pierre LeSoeur, an old adversary from Mickey's last lumber camp. He hadn't seen Pierre since he'd put the mark on him thirty years before.

A bearded man sitting next to Mickey shouted to the other end of the table, "Hey, Pierre, ol' pal. How about another round? We're gettin' thirsty down here."

"Oh, oui, monsieur. You just say the word, eh?" He raised his glass over his head. "Eh! Bebe!" he called to Judy as he pulled a fresh twenty from his shirt pocket. "Some drink for my friends."

The ten men squeezed in around the table and gave a cheer, their glasses raised to Pierre. Judy took their orders passing from one rowdy patron to the next. Each had started the evening drinking beer; but with Pierre picking up the tab, all had graduated to bourbon, rum, and whisky doubles.

Judy brushed past Mickey. He reached out and nearly crushed her wrist with his bare hand. "You have not taken my order, my little colleen. I am with these men, you know. You'll bring me a dram of your best Irish, won't you now, heh, heh."

Judy froze. Mickey's grip wrenched her arm. She winced in pain and looked nervously to the bar. Sam was busy at the other end. She glanced at Pierre. He set his jaw and shook his head as he slowly slid his chair behind him. "You will take your hand away from the lady, you worthless, Irish tramp. You think I don't remember you, eh?" He pointed to a deep scar on his left cheek. "Pierre remembers all too well that day in camp when the big Irish man beats up the young French-Canadian," Pierre snarled, rising to his feet. The Cedar Bar instantly fell still.

Mickey O'Flynn jumped to his feet. His chair flew out behind him as he pushed the petite waitress across the room. He reached for the scabbard on his left hip and pulled a knife, flashing it in the faint light. In a split second, every man in the bar leapt to his feet. The six closest grabbed Mickey by the arms and legs. The strongest, a six-foot, six-inch giant, took a strangle hold around Mickey's neck and nearly ripped his head from his shoulders.

Mickey croaked out to Pierre LeSoeur, "I should have killed you then when I had the chance."

The giant behind him tore the knife from Mickey's hand as Pierre pushed his way through the mass of men. He stood nose to nose with the Irishman. Staring him in the eye, Pierre scoffed, "Now that I am your size, I tell you this to your face. You could not fight your way out of the bottom of an outhouse, even if you wanted to, you stinking, Irish, shanty boy. Now, I will make you think twice before you harm anybody again." He looked at the men who held Mickey. "Let him stand on his own. I will beat him the way he beat me when I was a boy." Pierre glanced down and picked his target. Before Mickey could react, Pierre slammed a tremendous right fist deep into Mickey's belly.

Mickey gasped as he doubled over in agony. The six men grabbed him keeping him on his feet. Mickey shook his head, his face dangling inches from the floor. He snorted up a mouthful of bloody phlegm, straightened his back, and unloaded the slimy gob squarely in the middle of the Frenchman's face.

Pierre jumped back, snarled, and charged into Mickey O'Flynn. He slammed his fists like piledrivers into Mickey's belly. The Irishman slumped into unconsciousness. Pierre stood over his rival and placed one foot heavily on the side of Mickey's face. He leaned his weight on the middle of his foot and spun around once, twice, three times. A bright red welt immediately rose over Mickey's right cheekbone. It would be a mark the Irishman would carry for the rest of his life, one that would symbolize Pierre's vengeance for the one-sided battle of thirty years before.

"<u>Messieurs</u>, you will remove this lowlife from my sight," Pierre yelled.

The six men, three on a side, dragged Mickey along the floor while another opened the front door to Hodeck Street. They slid him over the boardwalk and deposited him on the edge of the dusty roadway. The biggest one tossed Mickey's knife and cap out in the dirt beside him.

———

It was nearly one a.m. before Mickey O'Flynn staggered to his feet. He heard Pierre and all the other men inside the Cedar Bar still laughing—laughing at him, he was sure. He picked up his knife and pulled down his cap before stumbling back to his canoe. By the time he'd paddled out of Cedarville Harbor, he'd decided he'd fix Pierre LeSoeur once and for all.

Mickey looked across Cedarville Channel to LaSalle Island. He listened for boats that might swamp his canoe in the open water. Seeing and hearing nothing, he cut across to the Elliot Hotel pier. His anger raged as he approached the LaSalle Island shore. Rather than going around the Elliot Hotel dock, he went through it between the fourth and fifth stone cribs. He passed three boathouses before coasting up to the abandoned, green one at the end of Elliot Bay.

As Mickey approached, he noticed that something was out of place. The left side of the boat entrance was wrenched up out of position. His canoe slid easily underneath. Either the boathouse had shifted since he'd left that afternoon or someone had broken in. Could the Frenchman have come from the bar ahead of Mickey to finish him off? Mickey moved ahead slowly.

31

He pulled a wooden match from his vest pocket, lit it, and detected the form of a large man huddled face down against the old canoe. It wasn't Pierre, that was for sure. He'd never seen this man before.

Mickey doused the light and pulled himself silently up on the deck. He unsheathed his hunting knife and moved ahead until he stood over the intruder. He struck another match. The large man jerked from his sleep in alarm.

Mickey stood, holding his blade over Fats' head. "What are you doing here?" Mickey bellowed.

Gerald FitzRoberts sat up, the match blazing in front of his eyes. The moon glistened on the water and flashed on the knife blade only inches from his throat.

"W-who are you?" Fats stammered.

"None of your business," Mickey yelled. "This is my place. How'd you get here?"

"Some French guy dropped me off at sundown," Fats said. His eyes slowly adjusted to the brightness of the match. He could tell the man before him was relatively small, save for the knife. Fats slowly brought his arms in front of him. "You take one move at me," Fats growled, "and you'll wish you hadn't."

Mickey stepped back. "We'll see about that," he said. "A Frenchman, you say." His match flickered. He flipped it into the water and lit another. "Aye, it all fits. You're the man they were talking about at the bar tonight. Your boat blew up in Bosely Channel yester-day chasing some rich kids from Mackinac. Well, Fat Man, you're in luck. They think you drowned and got washed out into the big lake."

"Is that right?" Fats growled. "What if I am? What's it to you?"

Mickey struck another match and stared at Fats for several moments. "I think we can work something out, FitzRoberts. That's your name, Gerald FitzRoberts?"

Fats hiked himself up and leaned against the wall. "Yeah, who are you?"

"It's Mickey O'Flynn, I am," the Irishman said, tugging his cap. "A lumbering man. Aye, we just might be able to work something out, the two of us. But we can't do it from here. If Frenchy knows you're here he just might send the sheriff after you. That wouldn't do, at all. No, we've got to move right now. And I've got just the place, a boathouse over on Little LaSalle. I heard about it tonight at the bar."

"What makes you think I'll help you?" Fats snarled.

"Oh, you will. You don't have a choice. You're a marked man, you are. You won't put a club up against the back of my head like you did that bloke on Mackinac," Mickey smiled a devilish grin and then grimaced, the pain of Pierre's coup de grace shooting through his cheekbone. "Aye, everyone's been talking about you. Those rich resort kids you let get away were strutting around town like they were some kind of national heroes. They told the cops about your counterfeit money scam. And Old Man Geetings? You only stunned him. The kids saved his worthless hide, and he's in jail. Everyone thinks you're dead. Most folks would be glad if you were. Not me, though. I've got a score to settle with that scurvy Frenchman, I do. Aye. It fits, all right," Mickey said more to himself than to Fats. "Frenchy stole some fake money from you, didn't he? I'll bet that's what he was using tonight at the bar— counterfeit twenties. I think we'd both like a shot at Frenchy. Am I right, Fats?"

33

"You'd better think again, Paddy. I'm not throwing in with the likes of you."

"You'd better understand something, Fats," Mickey sneered. "I'm your passport out of here. Your picture'll be in every newspaper and post office in the country. They'd string you up in a minute for what you did. When it comes time, I'll get you out of here. But not until. No, Fats—that's what they call you, right?—Fats? You're safe with me, Fats, and I'm safe with you. We're survivors, you and me. We'll get along just fine, won't we, Fats."

Fats leaned toward Mickey clenching his fist. "You call me `Fats' one more time, you scrawny little buzzard, and we'll see how long you survive, kapeesh?"

"Settle down, big fellow. We're in this together. Don't you forget that."

"Okay, Paddy," Fats continued, leaning back against the boathouse wall. "Let's get on with it."

"That's better," Mickey sneered. "Now, let's load the canoe. We're moving out before the fishermen roll in. There's plenty of moonlight to get us where we're going."

"The boathouse in Snows Channel should be well stocked by now."

CHAPTER 6
THE CHAPMAN BOATHOUSE

Tuesday, July 1 2:00 a.m.

Mickey O'Flynn handed Fats a paddle and then settled into the back of the canoe. With Fats in the bow and all the gear and supplies stowed in the middle, there was only about two inches of freeboard keeping them from capsizing. It did make sliding out of the boathouse somewhat easier, but the rest of the journey would be extremely hazardous. If one speedboat passed, even from across the bay, its wake would swamp the canoe; Fats and Mickey would sink like a couple of sledgehammers.

Once past Harold Geetings' island, Fats noticed some other landmarks that he'd become familiar with over the past two summers. In the distance he saw the flashing buoys at Connors Point and Middle Entrance, markers that he had followed in the black-hulled speedboat to Mackinac Island on his weekly counterfeit money runs.

The brilliant moon provided ample light for Mickey to guide his canoe along the shoreline. Around Urie

35

Point, he kept within a paddle's width of the tall reeds and followed the shoreline of Urie Bay. Staying close to land provided him the best cover from being seen as well as a fighting chance to save himself should a wave swamp his boat.

After crossing the narrow entrance of Bosely Channel, Mickey followed the shore to Arnold Point. There, a mansion of a boathouse stood magnificently with a commanding view of Muscallonge Bay, Elliot Bay, and Urie Bay. It towered over Fats and Mickey, its five separate openings affording shelter for an entire flotilla of sport and luxury vessels. All the portals, however, were closed, their doors reaching to within a foot of the water line. Mickey drew the bow of the canoe up to the smallest of the entrances.

"You'll have to raise the corner for us to get inside," Mickey said. "Careful now. Don't sink us."

Fats stood up and braced his left foot outside the canoe against the edge of the stone crib. He grasped a piling with his left arm and grabbed the door with his right hand. Straining, he wrenched the left hand side up eight inches higher than the right. The screech of the wood and metal echoed throughout Urie Bay.

"That should do it," Fats said sitting down. He pulled the canoe the rest of the way inside.

Mickey struck a match. Its faint glow illuminated the nearby area.

"Och, I have died and gone to heaven," Mickey said, his eyes flashing through the enormous building. Three mahogany inboards were stored high out of the water supported by several twelve-inch beams and chain winches. There was a small parlor set up nearby complete with a table, two chairs, and a refrigerator.

Fats detected the faint hum of its motor. "Hey, Mickey," he said warily, "are you sure no one's using this place?"

"Oh, aye, I heard them say so at the bar. Some rich Chicago family owns it. They won't be up all summer. The caretaker, an Indian named Jim Osogwin, left yesterday to be with his family north of the Sault for a fortnight. That should give us plenty of time."

"Yeah, well, what if the place has bats?" Fats argued.

"Och, and what if it does?" Mickey snorted. "It's a palace compared to what the sheriff will have for you. Now, let's settle in. We've got a few days to work on some plans for our French mate."

"What kind of plans are you talking about?" Fats growled.

Mickey leaned back in a dock chair touching gingerly the huge welt on his cheek. "I not sure just yet. But mark my words, I'll be wanting him to wiggle like a worm on a hook and to know that it's the Irishman what's getting his due. It won't be fast, you can be sure, and I don't want him returning the favor, if you get my message."

"You want me to put him away, is that right?"

"Aye. It makes sense to me," Mickey replied. "You've already laid one man low. What's one more? Besides me, Pierre's the only one that knows that you didn't meet your end in Bosely Channel, right?"

"Yeah, that suits me fine. I know some little brats I'd like to pay back, too," Fats whispered.

"Speak up, my stout friend. If you've got something to say, you'd best be saying it so's I can hear."

"Those kids I was chasing when my boat blew up live around here somewhere. Old Man Geetings told me so. I'd like to put them where they almost put me, on the bottom of Lake Huron."

"You'll best not be getting such grand ideas," Mickey warned. "If an old, French trapper disappears, who's to care. But if four rich, resort kids go missing, every cop in the state will be combing this area. They won't quit until we're in the hoosegow. You'd best forget that notion right now."

Fats made his way from the canoe to the top of the ladder. "Maybe so, but I'd sure like to give them a scare they won't forget."

"Aye, well, don't get carried away with it," Mickey said, staring at Fats, "or, for sure, we'll both be carried away because of it. Now, let's check out this rich man's barn."

"I don't know about you, Mickey, but I haven't eaten all day. I'm going to see what's in that fridge," Fats said. He opened its door; the light came on but nothing was there.

"All right," Mickey said. "There's a boathouse nearby on Snows Channel. I haven't hit it since last summer. It should be pretty well stocked by now. You stay here. I'll be back before sunrise."

Mickey stepped into the canoe and slid silently through the tilted boathouse door into Muscallonge Bay.

"I find a little envelope under a rock," Pierre told the sheriff.

CHAPTER 7
BACK IN TOWN . . . .

Tuesday, July 1 2:00 a.m.

"Oh, monsieur, it cannot be. The money, it must be real," Pierre pleaded with Sheriff Shoberg. "There is some mistake, non?"

"Look, Frenchy, I'm not in the mood for games. It's two in the morning. I've got to testify in St. Ignace at noon, so don't waste my time. Sam got me out of bed when he discovered that you'd been buying drinks for everyone with counterfeit twenties." The sheriff turned to the bartender. "Let me see those again, Sam." Sam Trefry handed him three twenty dollar bills. Con Shoberg spread them out in front of the Frenchman. "Now, Pierre," he said, "where'd you get this money?"

"Oh, oui, monsieur, THAT money," Pierre said, glancing nervously around the empty bar. "It is this way. I hear this afternoon about the old man in Elliot Bay. He was taken to prison, non? I go to his island to see what I can see. Maybe he leave something I can use. I am almost there when two policemen come out of the cabin and get in a boat. They drive away from

39

the dock—vroom. I wait, and when they are gone, I paddle ashore. I walk up to the cabin. The door, she is bolted, so I walk around the outside. I find a little envelope under a rock. Inside there are three twenty dollar notes."

"Found them under a rock, eh?" Sheriff Shoberg said, taking a set of handcuffs from his belt. He slapped them on Pierre's wrists and led him out of the tavern. They walked along Hodeck Street up to the Clark Township building. The sheriff unlocked the front door and ushered his prisoner through the darkened office to a small jail cell.

"One more chance, Pierre," the sheriff said. "You're sure there's no more?"

"Oui, monsieur, I swear. I bring all of them here and buy drinks for my friends."

"Well, I think we'd better take a little run out to your camp tomorrow. You still staying in that shack on Bass Cove Lake?"

"Oui, monsieur, but please, my place, she is a mess. Allow me to clean it up. You come tomorrow. We talk, oui?"

"No," the sheriff said. "Tonight, you're going to spend the night in a nice warm bed, compliments of Clark Township. I've got a room made up just for you. You like bars, don't you, Frenchy? This place has plenty of them. Tomorrow, if you don't remember a few more details about this counterfeit money, we'll take a ride out to your shack. Maybe look under a few rocks. If I find one piece of stolen property from one of the boathouses, I'll run you in for breaking and entering. You'll have a new, permanent address in St. Ignace, comprenney voo?"

Pierre understood. He had two choices. He could give up the treasure of fake twenties he still held in the seam of his jacket or he could wait until morning, go out with the sheriff to his shack where there was ample evidence of his robbing a dozen boathouses. Pierre needed a miracle. Maybe one would happen during the night. The hope of keeping the fortune in twenties was worth the chance.

"<u>Oui, monsieur. Bon soir</u>," he said, slumping onto the hard jail mattress.

At that, Sheriff Shoberg locked Pierre's cell door and headed across the street to his own bed.

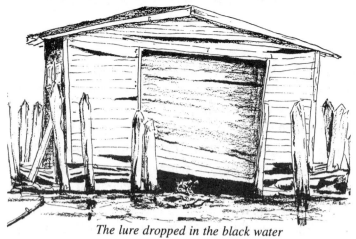

*The lure dropped in the black water
just inside the boathouse.*

CHAPTER 8
THE TROPHY

Tuesday, July 1, 4:30 a.m.

Morning came very quickly for Pete who was being nudged from the side of his bunk by his dad.

Not even the faintest sign of daylight peeked through the wavy windowpanes of his bedroom. Howard Jenkins had dressed, made breakfast, and started a fire in the wood stove to break the chill of the northern summer night.

"Rise and shine; it's daylight in the swamp," he leaned over and whispered into Pete's ear. "Time to call on our friends, Mr. Largemouth Bass and Mr. Northern Pike, to come out and play."

Pete was still dog-tired, but he knew that sunrise was the best hour to catch fish. By the time he'd dressed and had a bowl of cereal, the black of night would become the gray of dawn. He rolled out of the lower bunk and slipped into the same sweat socks, jeans, and tee-shirt he had pulled off the night before. In the dark he laced up his old, black basketball shoes and yanked the Michigan State College sweatshirt over his head. He felt his way along the wall, brushed aside the bedroom curtain, and stood in the living room by the wood stove. A kerosene lantern in the kitchen glowed, guiding him toward a bowl of diced bread and apples his dad had set for him. Pete added milk and sugar and sat at the table to eat.

After gulping down the homemade cereal and swigging the milk from the bottom of the bowl, he put on his fishing jacket. In minutes, he was following his dad down to the boat shed. They each grabbed a fishing pole and seat cushion. Pete also picked up the tackle box, and Mr. Jenkins carried the gas can out of the small building. They made their way down the hundred-foot long, two-plank wide, wooden dock out to the *Tiny Tin*, the Jenkins' aluminum fishing boat. Not a breath of wind disturbed Elliot Bay, the morning stars mirrored on its glassy surface.

"Let's just paddle over to Long's boathouse," Howard Jenkins said. "When the water's this still, a motor would spook every fish in the Snows."

Pete stepped into the bow; his dad sat in the stern where he normally ran the motor. This morning, though, Howard set the oars quietly in their oarlocks, pushed the boat away from the dock, and began to row along the outside of the reed bed.

Long's boathouse was the last one in the shallowest part of Elliot Bay. The dock that led to it had been broken up years ago by the ice, so it sat strangely isolated from the rest of civilization. It was halfway between Big LaSalle Island and Harold Geetings' tiny island. Pete glanced over at the writer's cottage and thought about the old man now in jail. He suddenly felt sorry for him. It was hard to imagine. Only yes-

43

terday Pete had feared Fats, now dead, and Mr. Geetings above any two people on earth. And why not? The two had come within inches of killing his sister, his three friends, and himself.

Pete glanced back at the old, green boathouse. The Long family hadn't come up to their cottage in a decade, and the years of neglect had taken its toll on the once sturdy boat shelter. Ice had lifted the pilings on one side giving the whole building a lopsided effect. What little paint remained was blistered and peeled. The brutal winter storms had stripped away most of the shingles and all of its shutters. It was on the verge of falling over.

Pete opened the tackle box and peered in for his favorite bass lure, a golden flatfish. Still too dark to see inside, he reached in his jacket pocket for his handy, pen-shaped flashlight and clicked it on. The battery was almost dead, but a faint beam reflected the glitter on his speckled lure. Pete tied it to his black line and cut the excess with his dad's old switch-blade hunting knife that Pete kept in the other pocket.

Howard Jenkins stopped rowing and lifted the oars out of the water. He set them quietly in the boat. He picked up his rod and reel and made a cast toward the reed bed in front of Mr. Geetings' island. Pete, facing the other way, couldn't help noticing that something was different about the dilapidated boathouse sixty feet in front of him. He flicked his flatfish directly toward the old building. The lure arced through the crisp morning air and dropped in the black water under the boathouse door, a foot inside. It was a perfect cast. Something should hit it. He retrieved his line slowly. Nothing did.

Behind him, Pete heard his dad's line whiz out again. Howard's Jitterbug splashed seductively on the edge of a lily pad.

Pete tried to see inside the boathouse, but all was black. The sun still hadn't poked over the horizon.

There's something different about that boathouse, Pete thought again. *What is it?* He made another cast just off to the side of the dock.

Twenty feet behind him, a tremendous splash startled Pete out of his reverie. He spun around to the stern and saw his dad holding his pole high in the air. The rod was bent double. A hefty bass was doing a tail walk across the water. The fish's mouth was gaping open as its entire body shook in monumental paroxysms of energy attempting to dislodge the barb from its lip. Keeping his eye on the show, Pete cranked his reel.

Suddenly, Pete's line jerked furiously. He spun his head to see a monstrous bass exploding out of the water. "I've got one!" he shouted. "He's huge!"

Instantly, the crank reversed in a blur. Yards of line screamed off Pete's reel as the bass shot across the boathouse entrance. It then plunged toward the bottom of the shallow bay, darting toward a thick growth of tall, green rushes.

There was no holding him back. Pete kept his thumb on the spool, but this baby was on a mission, and dinner at the Jenkins was not part of the agenda. Pete's thumb blistered as the black, five-pound test line zinged toward shore.

"If he gets into those reeds, you'll never get him out of there," his dad said, glancing over his shoulder. Howard was still playing his fish, but he could tell his son had a trophy. Mr. Jenkins hurried to bring his six-pounder up to the edge of the boat. He reached over the side, grabbed it by its lower jaw, and hauled it aboard. He snapped it to the chain stringer and turned to help Pete.

"My line's snarled in the reeds," Pete yelled. "I can't reel it in!"

"I'll row to the other side, Pete. Hold on!"

Howard Jenkins crammed the oars in their locks and thrust the *Tiny Tin* around the reed bed, but it looked as if Pete's bass had won the war. The line was completely tangled, and the fish swam thirty feet away splashing occasionally on the surface. It wouldn't take much to dislodge the small barb from its lip.

In the first rays of sunlight, Pete reached out and grabbed the black line from the far side of the reed bed. He wrapped the end closest to the tired bass around his arm several times; the fish tugged gently at his coat sleeve. Pete set the pole in the bottom of the boat, snatched the knife from his jacket pocket, and pressed the switch. The blade snapped into place. He quickly cut the line from where it came out of the reeds and also near the end of his pole. He tied the two ends and reeled in the line from around his arm. When Pete took up all the slack, the trophy fish felt the jerk from Pete's pole. He flew again into the air and charged, this time, for deeper water.

"He's still on!" Pete shouted.

"Be careful, don't horse him."

Pete reeled; slowly the knotted line fed into the spool. The bass came grudgingly, inch by inch, toward the boat. It swam from side to side in the black water. It made a turn and attempted a run, but it hadn't the strength to throw the hook. It came up to the *Tiny Tin* on its side. Pete's dad reached over, slipped his thumb into its soft, lower jaw, and lifted the monstrous fish into the boat. This wasn't a largemouth. It was a hogmouth!

"He's got to be ten pounds," Pete yelled as the sun broke the horizon.

Mr. Jenkins snapped it on the chain stringer. The two fish flopped, side by side, in the bottom of the *Tiny Tin.* Howard's bass, as big as it was, looked like bait.

"With all the commotion we've put up, we won't catch anything else around here," Pete's dad said. "Let's take him into town and get him weighed. I think you've just caught first prize in the bass contest, Pete. That Shakespeare rod and reel at the bait shop will be yours for sure."

"You really think so?" Pete laughed. "Wow!"

Howard Jenkins lifted the oars into the boat and pulled the starting cord on the blue, five-horsepower Chris-Craft motor. She caught on the third pull, and the *Tiny Tin* chugged across Elliot Bay toward Cedarville Channel.

During the twenty minutes of action, the reddish-gold sun had risen over LaSalle Island. As Mr. Jenkins directed the *Tiny Tin* along Cincinnati Row, Pete tried to see if there was any activity near Dan, Kate, and Eddie's boathouse. He hoped he'd be able to show off his fish, but there was no movement along the shoreline at all. He certainly couldn't see through the dense growth of birches and cedars where their large summer homes were concealed in privacy. It occurred to Pete, if he ever had a place like theirs, he'd want to show it off to everyone in the world. He certainly wouldn't hide it behind a bunch of old trees. Sometimes he couldn't figure these Cincinnati Row people out at all.

Pete's dad guided the boat across Cedarville Bay and pulled up to the Rainbow Bait And Tackle dock. Pete hopped out and hurried along the short pier carrying the two bass while his dad tied the boat to the pilings. Pete went in the back door. Mrs. Smith took one look and jumped right out of her chair.

"Look at this!" she exclaimed. "Where'd you get him?"

"Down in Elliot Bay," Pete grinned. He immediately realized the error of divulging his secret. "Er, ah, down that way . . . sort of, you know, between there and, uh, . . . Goose Island. My dad and I brought him in to be weighed for the contest."

"There's nothing close, I can tell you that," Donna Smith bubbled. "Bring him over here. We'll just unsnap him and put him on the scale. There we go." She dropped Pete's bass in the metal basket. The needle cranked over. "Ten pounds, seven and . . . one-half ounces," she said. "Nobody'll touch that, son. Elliot Bay, eh? What'd you say you got him on?"

"Um, I didn't, ma'am," Pete said, glancing down at the floor. "And if it's all the same, I'd just as soon not."

Donna Smith was always trying to find out where the big ones were being caught and what they were hitting on so she could pass along the information to her best customers. All it would take would be one slip of the tongue, and Elliot Bay would be shore-to-shore bass fishermen casting golden flatfish at sunrise for the rest of the summer.

"Fine by me," she said. "All I need's your name and where I can reach you next Friday. Thursday, July the tenth at sundown, that's the end of the bass contest. Say, aren't you Howard Jenkins' boy? Wasn't it you that brought in that big muskie a couple of weeks ago?"

"That's right, ma'am. I'm Pete Jenkins."

"Well, Pete Jenkins, I'd say you're having yourself some kind of summer."

"Sure am," Pete said as his dad came in the back door.

"Howard," Donna Smith said. "I didn't even recognize Pete, he's grown so. Now, Pete, step outside. I've got to take a picture of you and your fish for the Weekly Wave. I'll give it to the Shakespeare people for advertising if you win the rod and reel. Fact is, I wouldn't be surprised if you won top prize in all of Michigan."

As Mrs. Smith snapped the picture, the shutter opened and closed.

"That's it!" Pete whispered to his dad. "That's what was different about Long's boathouse."

"What do you mean?" Howard Jenkins asked.

"The boathouse entrance—it was partially opened, cockeyed. It's been closed for years with the door right down to the water. I made my first cast this morning with my flatfish going right into the boathouse."

"A flatfish, eh?" Mrs. Smith smiled. "At the old Long's boathouse, you say. What color did you use?"

"Let's go, Pete," Howard Jenkins said with a wink to Donna, "before Mrs. Smith finds out you had bread and milk with diced apples for breakfast."

"No, really," Pete pressed, his face flushing in embarrassment. "How come that door is open at the boathouse?"

"It's just ice damage from last winter, Pete. Ice forces the pilings up each year; if no one takes care of them, they'll eventually come right out of the water. Pretty soon, the whole thing falls over. You've just been so busy with everything else this summer that you haven't noticed. Tell you the truth, I hadn't either. Now, let's head home so I can show off my big bass."

"YOUR big bass," Pete questioned.

"Yes, MY big bass. Of course, I'll have to walk up the hill first before anyone sees yours, but that six-pounder is the biggest one I've caught in years. Let's go. 'Bye Donna."

"'Bye, Howard," Mrs. Smith said. "Thanks for all the info, Pete," she smiled. "I'll see to it that you won't be lonely down in Elliot Bay for the rest of the summer. Say, it wasn't that speckled, golden flatfish I sold your dad last year, was it?"

At that, Pete tripped and almost fell in the water as he made his way along the dock to the *Tiny Tin*.

The phone inside the Rainbow Bait office rang. Donna Smith laughed as she waved to Howard and hurried to answer it.

*"There's been two more boathouse break-ins,"
Sheriff said.*

CHAPTER 9
THE SUSPECTS

Tuesday, July 1 8:00 a.m.

"Get up, Frenchy," Sheriff Shoberg said as he turned the jail cell key. "I just got another phone call. There's been two more boathouse break-ins. Sam Trefry says that you were at the Cedar Bar all afternoon and evening, so I guess that lets you off the hook. Saves me from searching your miserable campsite, too. But if you find any more twenty dollar bills under any more rocks, you bring them to me, comprenney voo?"

"Oui, monsieur. Merci, merci." *It's a miracle! What an unbelievable stroke of luck. Someone else must be filching food from boathouses besides me,* Pierre LeSoeur thought. *It is probably that low-life, Irish lumberjack, Mickey O'Flynn.*

Sheriff Shoberg pulled the cell door open; and Pierre LeSoeur scrambled out of the narrow, single bunk bed. He felt in his jacket lining for the lump of counterfeit twenties and smiled to himself as he walked—danced, really—in front of Betty Schoolcraft into the morning sunshine. He hurried along Hodeck

51

Street past the Bon Air to Cedarville Bay. He pushed away a blanket of reeds that covered his canoe and slipped quietly out of the harbor. He paddled around the west side of LaSalle Island, through Bosely Channel, and along the Lake Huron shoreline to his shack on Bass Cove Lake.

———

"Betty?" Sheriff Shoberg called into the front office.

"Yes, Con?" Mrs. Schoolcraft replied.

"Would you get the word around for anyone who sees Mickey O'Flynn to call me? If the burglar isn't Frenchy, then I'm stumped if it isn't the old Irishman. I'll keep an eye on Joseph Red Owl, too, but I don't think it's him. He may be an outcast from the local Ojibwas, but he doesn't strike me as a common thief. People keep telling me they've seen Mickey O'Flynn from a distance but never long enough to get a fix on where he's staying. I heard he was canned from his job at the quarry some time ago. Call Donna Smith down at Rainbow Bait. Ask her to have her customers to be on the lookout for him. Especially the late night and early morning trade. Mickey must be moving around staying in different places." Con strapped on his shoulder holster and grabbed his hat. "Sam Trefry told me Mickey was at the Cedar Bar last night, so I know he's around."

"All right, Con," Betty said. "I'll get to it right now."

"I'm leaving for the Geetings' preliminary hearing in St. Ignace," Sheriff Shoberg continued. "I probably won't be back until after you leave the office tonight. You know where to reach me if anything happens, okay?"

"Ten-four, Con. See you tomorrow."

Pete and his dad pushed away from the Rainbow Bait dock.

CHAPTER 10
THE BREAK-IN

Tuesday, July 1   8:10 a.m.

It was just after eight when Pete and his dad pushed away from the Rainbow Bait dock and rode along Cedarville Channel past the red, double boathouse. Pete looked but didn't really expect to see any activity on Cincinnati Row. No one along there ever moved before nine. Glancing through the trees toward the Hinken's cottage, however, Pete was reminded of all the mounted wildlife decorating their living room walls. For each animal there was a fabulous story of how Dan's father captured this bear in Timbuktu or his grandfather shot that tiger in the wilds of Borneo. The Les Cheneaux Islands might not be as exotic as any of those places, nor his fish as ferocious as any of those wild beasts but, all in all, this was a pretty good story. And it was a prize-winning bass. Or soon would be.

"Hey, Dad. How about we get this baby stuffed?" Pete called out over the steady, waa-waa-waa of the one-cylinder motor.

Mr. Jenkins guided the *Tiny Tin* around the Elliot Hotel pier. He eased the throttle lever to the left as they cruised up to their dock. "Oh, Pete," his dad said, "you wouldn't want to do that to a poor, defenseless fish, would you? Let's just eat him. Besides, taxidermy is real expensive. I bet it would cost fifty dollars to be mounted."

"No kidding? Fifty dollars? Maybe we'll just take pictures." *Holy cow,* Pete thought. *Those trophies at the Hinken's must have cost a fortune. Then again, that should be no surprise. Everything anyone does along Cincinnati Row is done with no expense spared.* Pete got to thinking how lucky he was just to have the cabin they had. His mom inherited it from Grandma Heidelberg who wasn't even really related but had been a longtime family friend with no heirs. Pete's mom had spent all of her young adult summers staying with her in the Snows, helping around the cottage. When Grandma Heidelberg died, two years before Pete was born, Pete's mom was named in her will to take over the cottage. It was like a gift from God. Better than money. So, Pete, a very ordinary kid, spent every summer in one of the world's most exclusive resort areas. He fished and swam in crystal clear waters off cedar green islands under dazzling blue skies. Meanwhile, back in Saginaw, all of his school friends sweated out one flat summer after another doing just about anything to find some shade. Pete was a lucky kid, and he knew it.

They docked the *Tiny Tin*, and Pete followed his dad up the hill to the cottage. Pete found his mom and sister reading on the front porch. Mrs. Jenkins took one look at the stringer and jumped up to get the

Brownie camera. The two fishermen walked around the cottage and posed at the back stoop wash stand with their bass. Then they hiked another thirty yards into the woods to the fish cleaning station. Pete scaled and his dad filleted. Mr. Jenkins cut open the fishes' stomachs to see what their catch had been feeding on. Inside the big one were two crabs, a frog, and a blue gill: a pretty nourishing breakfast, that is, until he'd chosen a speckled golden flatfish for dessert.

———

It was about two in the afternoon when Pete started down to Cincinnati Row in the *Tiny Tin*. Pete saw Kate wading along the beach by the red, double boathouse. Her dazzling smile and summer tan drew him like a playful puppy to a furry kitten.

"Pete!" she exclaimed as he cut the motor and drifted toward her. "Am I glad to see you! We need your help. Our boathouse was robbed last night. My change purse was stolen, and our refrigerator was broken into. All the beach food was taken."

"Beach food?" Pete asked.

"Yes, you know, pop, beer, bread, cheese. Stuff like that."

"You've got a refrigerator in your boathouse?" Pete didn't even have one in his cottage. Just an old ice box. That's why he and his sister went to town every day, to get ice. That and to get mail and to go to the Bon Air for his Holloway Slo-Poke. It wasn't all bad, mind you. But a refrigerator in a boathouse? What would these Cincinnati people think of next?

"There have been petty thefts around here all summer," Kate added. "But this is the first one along Cincinnati Row. We've heard other people talking about

55

them, but we were so busy spying on Harold Geetings that I guess we didn't pay any attention. But now that it's happened to us, well, that changes everything. It's such a creepy feeling knowing that someone was standing right here last night stealing our stuff."

Pete took his stern line and threw a double half hitch onto a dock piling. "Any idea who's doing it?" he asked.

"Could be anyone, but my dad thinks it's kids. Probably looking for beer, he says," Kate replied. "He called the sheriff. Mr. Shoberg said it's been mostly right around Cedarville along the mainland and the nearby islands. But it's always boathouses, never cottages. And all that's ever taken is food and things like that. Nothing that can be traced."

Just then, Eddie and Dan walked down the dock, "Hi, Pete. I hope you got plenty of sleep last night," the fresh-faced, blond-haired Dan said. "We've got work to do."

Dan, Kate, and Pete had all just turned fifteen. Kate and Dan were twins, each was tall and slim, Kate an inch or two shorter than Dan, who was about 5'9", the same as Pete. Neither Pete nor Dan had reached his full height. Kate, on the other hand, had attained perfection. Pete often became totally distracted just thinking about her.

Eddie was almost sixteen but was much bigger— over six feet tall, and as strong as a tugboat. He had dark, curly hair, sparkling eyes, and a deep, almost incessant, good-natured laugh. All three spoke with a wonderful, southern Ohio accent, a marvelously musical, soft-spoken drawl. By comparison, Pete thought he sounded like one of Ming's robots in the Flash Gordon movies. Kate, Dan, Eddie and all their friends, even the little kids, conducted themselves with confidence and grace and polished sophistication far beyond their years. Pete was awed by their every movement and mannerism—particularly Kate's.

"We were up all night after the boathouse was broken into," she said excitedly. "We couldn't sleep thinking about it."

"It appears that we have a brand new mystery to solve," Dan smiled. "What do you say, Pete, are you in?"

Pete stared dumbfounded at the three. As much as he wanted to be included in their activities, he slowly shook his head. "I don't know. I'm not all that anxious to rush into another deal like we did with Fats and Mr. Geetings. We could have been killed, you know. I can't believe you would want to risk something like that again."

Pete handed his bow line to Eddie and jumped up on the dock. "Look, I just caught a ten-and-a-half-pound bass this morning," he said thoughtfully. "I might have even won a brand new rod and reel in the process. When my dad and I came by this morning, I'd have shown you the fish, but I thought you'd all be asleep. I really enjoyed that, you know, fishing with my dad and all." Pete shook his head again. "You guys can do what you want about this boathouse thing, but I'm not ready to stick my neck out for a little excitement."

"Oh, come on, Pete," Kate said. "We're a team. You can't go into a shell now. We need you."

"That's right," Dan urged. "If we can track down a murderer and solve a counterfeit money scheme, a little soda pop and lunchmeat thief won't even be a contest."

"I don't know," Pete said, "if my mom or dad think

for one minute that I'm doing anything that might be dangerous, they'll lock me in the outhouse for the rest of the summer. I'd be cooped up with nothing but comic books and *Collier's* magazines with my sister right outside the door making sure I don't leave the whole time. You guys might know what it's like being grounded to your room, but not to an outhouse. I can tell you this, it ain't exactly 'Paris Nights' in there."

"All right," Eddie laughed. "We get the Kodak. But we're not asking you to keep anything from them. Besides, we need you. You're part of the team. You can't expect the rest of us to just ignore this. Our boat-house was broken into. Our stuff was stolen. Our integrity has been besmirched," he said, waving his arms dramatically.

"The entire Les Cheneaux resort community is depending on us," Dan added. "By Jove, we must get to the bottom of this. Think of our image," he added, striking a Sherlock Holmes pose with an imaginary magnifying glass.

"Well, since you put it that way," Pete said with a touch of sarcasm, "I suppose it's okay. All right, count me in, but if it comes to even a hint of danger, we tell our parents, agreed?"

"Great, Pete," Kate said anxiously. "Now, let's get a list of what's been taken from all the other boat-houses. We'll start by asking the kids at the Bon Air."

"First," Dan said, "we need to talk about the pot-luck party at our boathouse tomorrow night. Do you think you'll be able to come, Pete?"

"I'll have to ask my parents. What's it all about?"

"It's a dinner party we have every week," Dan replied. "There are about ten of us and we take turns hosting it. It's at a different boathouse every Wednesday. We cook out and set up tables on the beach. We have dinner, and then we have a campfire and talk and sing and stuff. We've got a lot to tell this time, and we want you to be there to give your part of the Geetings' story."

"The host is in charge of the main dish," Kate continued, "and everyone else brings something to pass—a salad, vegetable, or dessert. And the host can invite a guest. We'd like you to come. You won't have to bring anything. We always have more than we can eat."

"It's a camp out, too," Eddie said. "The guys bring sleeping bags and sack out on shore. If it looks like rain, we set up in the boathouse. The girls stay in the host's cottage. What do you say, Pete? Do you think your parents will let you?"

"When they find out about the break-ins I'll bet they won't be too thrilled," Pete replied. "But it wouldn't hurt to ask. The potluck and the party sound really fun." Pete hesitated. "I might need someone to help me explain it to them, though. Would one of you mind coming down to my place?"

"We all will," Kate offered at once. "None of us have ever been along Elliot Row. What do you say, guys?"

"We don't have to tell them about the break-ins, do we?" Dan smiled to Pete. "At least, not yet."

"You're trying to get me into some serious trouble," Pete laughed. "Look, I can do that all on my own."

All four piled into the red and white Lyman. Dan pulled the starter cord, and they were off to Elliot Bay.

Joseph Red Owl disappeared through a wall of rushes.

CHAPTER 11
JOSEPH RED OWL

Tuesday, July 1 3:30 p.m.

A half an hour later the four trotted down the stairs from Pete's cabin. Mr. and Mrs. Jenkins had given Pete permission to attend Dan and Kate's potluck the next night.

"You've got the greatest cottage, Pete," Eddie said as the four made their way down the stone path to Pete's dock. "It's like living in another century. You actually use candles and kerosene lanterns to read at night?"

"Yeah, pretty much," Pete nodded, a little embarrassed about the Spartan nature of his modest cabin. It was nothing like the fabulous ones along Cincinnati Row, some with more floors than his had rooms.

"I bet it's great playing cards and telling stories without radios and record players blasting all the time," Kate added.

"I suppose," Pete said, surprised at his friends' favorable assessment.

"It must be so private," Dan continued, "living here without people always calling you on the telephone."

"Plus, without any plumbing, I'll bet you're never bothered by dripping faucets," Eddie laughed.

"I guess I hadn't thought about that, either," Pete agreed.

"And even your boathouse is different," Dan said as the four stood in front of the old shed near the beach. "It's not in the water. I hate being in ours when we're having a sleep-over. I stay awake all night afraid I'll roll into the lake and drown."

"Hey, I've got an idea," Kate said. "Maybe next week we can have the potluck party at your place. It's scheduled for Sandy Chapman's boathouse on Little LaSalle, but I don't think she's coming up this year. All our friends really like it when we do things a little differently. What do you say, Pete?"

Pete didn't even know he had a boathouse. He'd never thought of the shack along the shore as being anything more than an old shed. Once the outboard had been hauled out for the summer, it did leave quite a bit of open space; but to call it a boathouse? It was nothing like the magnificent structures along Cincinnati Row with their massive stone cribs and wide docks. Many had attached beach houses and lavish guest rooms on the second floor.

Pete knew his family's cabin was less than adequate even compared to their boathouses. Still, for some reason, they wanted everyone to come to his place for next week's potluck. He always liked his cottage just fine. It had everything he ever wanted, but he never thought anyone would be impressed by it, especially the Cincinnati Row kids. He stopped and turned as the others made their way along the dock. Maybe it <u>was</u> special not having electricity or plumbing or anything.

"Well, I'm just glad you three came along," he said, catching up with Kate. "I needed all of you to talk them into letting me go to your potluck. Especially with Cara right there reminding them that if she'd done what I did on Mackinac Island, she'd have been grounded for life."

Dan smiled, putting his arm around Pete's shoulder. "Maybe we should allow your parents a few days before we suggest having the next party at your place, Pete. I've observed over the years that parents, in general, are a lot like desperate criminals—they don't react favorably to sudden moves."

"Now that we've got tomorrow settled, let's get to the Bon Air and start asking around about the burglaries," Eddie recommended.

"I think we should go to the police station first," Kate said. "Someone there could give us a list of the boathouses that have been broken into. Maybe we could find a pattern or something."

Dan nodded. "The sheriff might have even caught the guy by now. You coming, Pete?"

"We're just checking things out, right?" Pete asked.

"Right," Dan assured him. "Just asking questions."

They hopped into Dan's boat. In five minutes, they were pulling up to the city dock.

As they walked towards town, Pete noticed an old, hand-made canoe stowed in the reeds along the shoreline. "I wonder where that came from," he said, nudging Dan. "It looks as if it was just dropped off from the eighteenth century." As soon as he said it, he thought about his own cottage.

"I've never seen it around here before," Dan agreed. "It's old but it's well made. See how the joints are lashed with small hemlock roots? And the bottom is dry as tinder. I bet she can move."

The four passed Hossack's General Store and the Bon Air. They turned right on Meridian Road and came up to a one story, white-framed building with "Clark Twp." painted in black letters over the door. The dry heat of the July afternoon pressed down on the young resorters. They were less than a block from the waterfront, but the temperature was at least ten degrees higher than on the water. As they approached the building, the office door flew open. A thin, bronze-skinned young man with long, glistening black hair exploded out toward them. He was wearing leather moccasins, faded blue jeans, a black, long-sleeved shirt, and an expression of rage that burrowed into Pete's eyes and made him jump back. The young man brushed past them, practically knocking Pete off his feet.

"Who was that?" Eddie asked.

"I don't know, but he sure seemed anxious to leave the township office," Dan replied, holding the door open for the other three. They walked in and stood before a woman at the reception desk. She was filing papers into a wooden cabinet.

"Excuse me," Kate said. "Who can we talk to about the boathouse break-ins?"

A ceiling fan whirled over Betty Schoolcraft's head. She turned and looked up at the four youths. "The sheriff," she answered, eyeing the teenagers with suspicion. "He's in St. Ignace, right now. Why do you want to know?"

"Some things were stolen from our place last night, and we want to know if the person's been caught," Dan replied.

"Where's your boathouse?" Mrs. Schoolcraft asked.

"Big LaSalle, Cincinnati Row," Dan said. "My father, Dr. Hinken, called you this morning to make the report. He asked us to come in and see if you have caught the man yet."

She shuffled some papers, pulled a file out of a cabinet, and asked, "What's your last names?"

"Hinken," Dan repeated. "This is my sister, Kate, and this is Eddie Terkel. He's our neighbor. This is Pete Jenkins. He's from down past the Elliot."

"Well, I guess I can tell you," Mrs. Schoolcraft said, holding a manilla folder. "No one's been arrested so far, but Sheriff Shoberg has several suspects. Joseph Red Owl is one. He just left here. He wasn't very happy about it, but I think I convinced him that the sheriff is watching him. Pierre LeSoeur could be responsible for some of the burglaries. He was in jail last night, though. He's got a shack on Bass Cove Lake. Then there's Mickey O'Flynn. He's been seen in the area, but no one can say where he's staying. All three live like civilization doesn't apply to them. And as far as any of them being partners in this, there's even less of a chance for that. They're all loners—wouldn't give anyone the time of day, even if they knew. How they live from one year to the next is a mystery to me. Mr. Shoberg's not ruling out that it might be kids doing it; that's what I think. I'll bet it's kids. You hear or see anything, you let us know—pronto. I'll tell you this, I wouldn't mess with any of those first three I told you about, whether they're involved in the boathouse burglaries or not."

"Okay," Eddie said. "We'll let our parents know."

The four friends turned and left the Clark Township building and stood outside by the dusty road.

"Come on," Dan said. "Let's get back to the dock and see if that old canoe is still there. My guess is that it belongs to Joseph Red Owl."

They turned and hurried into town to the city dock. The canoe was gone.

"He couldn't have gone far," Eddie said. "Let's see if we can find him."

All four ran out to the end of the pier and jumped into Dan's boat.

"Down there," Kate pointed into the bay. "He's heading for the reeds by the lumber yard."

The canoe skimmed the water and disappeared through a wall of green rushes along the mainland shoreline. It left not so much as a broken reed in its wake.

"We don't dare follow him in there," Dan said. "He could just be waiting to see if anyone was following him. When he left the township office it didn't look as if he was in the mood for visitors. He could slit our throats and scalp us before we knew it."

"For all we know, he might be camping along that shore," Eddie said. "I've never been back in there. Have you, Pete?"

"Nope," Pete shook his head. "And I can't imagine anything along that stretch but mosquitoes and musk-rats. Hardly a place to set up camp."

"Wouldn't be a bad hiding place, though," Dan said. "If I were down on my luck and wanted some easy pickings, I might set up here, close to town. Plus, I'd be on the water where I wouldn't leave any tracks to my hideout."

"Sheriff Shoberg told my dad that all the break-ins were near Cedarville either on the mainland or the nearby islands," Kate said.

"That's right," Eddie agreed. "Joseph Red Owl gets my vote for Les Cheneaux Boathouse Burglar. Let's stick around awhile and see if he comes out of there."

"I've got to get home," Pete remembered. "Cara and I haven't gone grocery shopping yet. Besides, I think I'd better tell my parents about all this."

"Okay, Pete," Dan consented. "We'll spin you back. You can tell your parents if you have to, but I'm going to wait until we get a little more information before I get my folks too riled up. What do you think, Eddie?"

"I'll buy that, Dan," Eddie said with a wink to Kate. "If my parents find out I'm nosing into this boathouse thing, they'll be watching every move I make for the rest of the summer."

"That's right," Kate nodded back to Eddie. "If our folks have any idea that it's not just kids that are doing the break-ins, we won't be allowed to even look outside after sunset. That would be the end of the potlucks and everything else."

"All right," Pete said, rolling his eyes. "I get the message. I'll keep quiet. But if we see Joseph Red Owl or anyone else with anything that even remotely looks as if it was stolen from anybody's boathouse, that's it. We all tell everyone. Agreed? What is it with you three? You got some kind of death wish or something?"

Kate wrapped her arms around Pete. "We knew we could count on you. This will be the most fun ever. You'll see."

Dan pulled the starter cord and the red and white boat took off across Cedarville Bay to the red, double boathouse in Cincinnati Row. Pete hopped in the *Tiny Tin*, waved to his friends, and headed home.

66

The boat continued <u>beneath</u> the Elliot Dock.

CHAPTER 12
CINCINNATI ROW POTLUCK

Wednesday, July 2 6:00 p.m.

The next evening Pete steered the *Tiny Tin* up to the red, double boathouse and tossed his bow line to Dan. Dan put a couple of half-hitches to the closest dock piling and took the glass bowl covered with waxed paper that Pete handed him.

"What's this, Pete?"

"Ambrosia Salad, my favorite. It's got marshmallows, coconut, mandarin oranges, grapes—and it's all mixed up in sour cream."

"Sounds great, Pete," Kate said, "but you didn't have to bring anything. You're the guest."

"I know, but you don't know my mom. Even when she packs my lunch for school, she puts something in to share, an apple, an orange, a cupcake—something. There is practically no chance that I would have gotten beyond the front porch without a dish to pass. Besides, if no one else wants it, I could eat the whole thing myself."

"Oh, I don't think there'll be any problem with that," Dan said, peeking under the waxed paper.

Pete climbed up to the dock and heard a low, rumbling sound. He turned and saw the *White Cap*, a powerful, mahogany speedboat carrying two boys and two girls bearing down on and completely dwarfing the *Tiny Tin*.

"Whoa, Neal!" Duke called out. "There's a boat in front of us!"

The engine thundered in reverse and the *White Cap* slipped neatly alongside the dock, just nudging the *Tiny Tin*.

"I saw it," a well-muscled, towheaded boy scowled as he stepped from behind the wheel. "You think I can't handle this baby? I've been driving the *'Cap* since I was five."

Duke was first to jump onto the dock putting a bow line to a piling.

"Pete, you know Duke Armour from the softball game," Dan said. The slightly older and much taller Duke Armour smiled and reached out to shake Pete's hand. "Duke, Pete Jenkins," Dan concluded.

"Hi, Pete," Duke smiled. "Nice to see you again."

Pete returned the grip and nodded to his teammate who had pitched the resorters to their victory over the Cedarville squad.

"And this is Neal Preston from Little LaSalle Island," Dan said, turning to the driver of the *White Cap*. "He just came up this week. Neal, this is Pete Jenkins from Elliot Bay."

Neal jumped onto the dock his long blond, almost white hair flowing in the breeze. He brushed past Pete taking the stern line to a piling. He turned and faced Dan. Neal had bushy white eyebrows, pink cheeks, and a powerful chin. His features were regal and yet peculiar at the same time.

Pete smiled and offered his right hand to the newcomer.

"So this is Pete Jenkins," Neal said, eyeing Pete scornfully. "Yeah, I heard about you." He turned from Pete to Dan leaving Pete's right hand dangling momentarily in mid-air. Pete put it to use quickly scratching the back of his head.

"Duke tells me I've missed some excitement, " Neal continued to Dan. "What gives this year? I arrive two days ago and already our boathouse gets looted."

"You were broken into in Bosely Channel?" Dan asked in surprise. "That's a long way from Cedarville."

"Of course, in Bosely Channel," Neal snapped. "That's where it's been for the past fifty years. Where else would it be? Tell me," Neal said, squinting at Dan. "Was this a particularly hard winter for you people? Everyone's brains seem to have seized up or something. What does Cedarville have to do with it? The guy obviously has transportation. He could be stealing from any boathouse he wants to."

"Yes, I guess so," Dan said, ignoring the sarcasm. "But so far they've all been near town. We kind of suspected a certain Indian in a canoe, that's all. Bosely Channel's kind of remote for traveling without a motor."

"Whatever," Neal said, shaking his head and looking toward shore. "Hey, I'm starved. What's holding up the show? Come on, let's eat."

"Relax, Neal," Eddie laughed as he escorted another guest down the dock to the boathouse. "Pete, I'd like you to meet Ann Early. Ann, this is Pete Jenkins. Ann has a place down at the end of Cincinnati Row toward the Elliot."

"Hi, Pete," Ann smiled. Pete nodded nervously.

"We're just waiting for Peggy and John to arrive from Boot Island," Eddie continued. "John called from Peggy's saying they'd be a little late. Here, Neal, these should tide you over. Ann made them herself." Eddie set a plate of steaming, crabmeat-filled mushrooms on the shoreside dining table.

"Oh, Pete," Dan said as he noticed the two girls standing stiffly by the side of the *White Cap*. "Have you met Stella and Jane? Stella Moore, Jane Blair, I'd like you to meet Pete Jenkins," Dan said easily. "Pete's from Elliot Bay. Stella and Jane are from Club Point down Snows Channel."

"Hi," Pete mumbled, glancing again at his feet.

"Here they come," Kate announced, looking along the channel toward town. Pete recognized the blue-hulled Chris-Craft. It was the *Sea Wolf*. Her engine went from a high-pitched whine to a low rumble as its captain throttled her down in front of Heuck's boathouse.

"Ahoy, diners. <u>Bon appetit</u>," Peggy Altmeier called out, radiating enthusiasm as the large inboard approached. "It's time to PARTY!"

John Williams, the dark-haired *Sea Wolf* captain, nosed his boat carefully up to the dock. "Good evening," he said with a pleasant smile to his Les Cheneaux friends. "I hope we didn't detain you. If so, it was entirely my fault." For a fifteen year old, John could have passed for fifty.

"Nonsense!" Peggy laughed as she hopped ashore. "John arrived at my place in plenty of time. I just couldn't do a thing with my hair. I'd been snorkeling all afternoon and time just caught up with me. Who's this?" she said, smiling at Pete.

"Peggy, this is my friend, Pete Jenkins," Dan said. "Pete, this is Peggy Altmeier. She's from Chicago. Her parents have a summer home on Boot Island. Pete's from Elliot Row here on Big LaSalle. And, Pete, this is John Williams from Coryell Island. John, I'd like you to meet Pete Jenkins."

"So good to meet you, Pete," John said amiably as he extended his right hand. John looked as though he might be more comfortable in a three-piece suit.

"Well, everybody's here," Eddie said. "I'll get the meat from the boathouse fridge. Dan, you and Pete can pull the corn out of the fire."

Dan and Eddie had dug a pit in the beach, filled it with charcoal, and set a large iron grate over it. They had wrapped corn-on-the-cob and potatoes in tin foil and set them around the outside to bake. The coals glowed yellow-red, perfect for grilling the steaks.

Eddie came out of the boathouse with a large bundle wrapped in butcher paper and set it on a table. "Pick one to your liking," he called out.

In moments, everyone had gathered around, chosen a steak, and put it on the grill. Pete watched and followed everything Dan and Eddie did except Eddie liked his steak rare and Dan waited until his was well-done. Pete had no idea how he liked his, so when Kate took hers off, Pete did the same. Eddie gave him a fork and a wood-handled, serrated knife. Pete sat with Kate and Eddie at the long picnic table on the lawn just a few feet from the beach. Pete took his first bite of the <u>filet mignon</u>—it was as tender as a two-minute marshmallow and almost as sweet.

———

The sun was setting when Mrs. Hinken walked along the trail carrying a three-tiered, red, white, and blue cake. "Here you go, kids," she said. "Straight from the Hessel Bakery—a Fourth of July, American birthday cake."

Dr. Hinken followed with an armful of fireworks. "Okay," he said, "I know it's not quite the Fourth of July yet, but this is just to get everyone in the mood. Don't worry, though. We're still planning the big fireworks party over at Sand Bay."

For the next hour everyone took turns shooting bottle rockets and Roman candles into the channel.

———

Kate looked up into the starlit sky. A bank of ominous black clouds rose over the western horizon. "It looks like rain," she said to Stella. "I say we leave the boys to fend for themselves down here, and we move up to the cottage."

"Kate's right," Dan said, noting a distant flash of lightning. "Suppose we get the sleeping bags set up in the boathouse, guys. Eddie and I will put the fire out— if the rain doesn't beat us to it."

The girls filed up to the Hinken's cottage, and the boys carried their sleeping bags into the red, double boathouse. Shortly after they'd all settled in, the rain began, slowly at first, and then in buckets. Thunder rumbled nearby. The six boys told their best jokes and scariest stories with Pete and Dan stretched out on the floor of the *Polly Ann* and the others spread out around the dock. One by one, the steady drone of rain on the boathouse roof lulled them all to sleep.

———

The air was cool and damp when a bump of the *Polly Ann* against the boathouse awakened Pete. He opened his eyes. He was startled by the unfamiliar sensation that his bed could be moving beneath him. He sat up and looked over the stern of the *Polly Ann* slowly remembering where he was. The rain had stopped, and the skies had cleared. The crescent moon glowed brightly over the channel. Along the far shore, the wake of a small boat caught the silvery glint of the moon's reflection on the glassy water. Pete squinted, trying to see what could be making the waves. There, just outside the line of reeds, Pete caught the flash of a paddle near Islington Point. He nudged Dan's sleeping bag. Dan awakened quickly, sat up, and joined Pete looking over the stern of the *Polly Ann*.

"What's up?" Dan asked, blinking.

"Over there," Pete said. "It's a canoe. You don't suppose it's Joseph Red Owl, do you?"

"Could be," Dan yawned. "Is anyone with him?"

"Nope. Not that I can see. What time is it?"

"Can't read my watch," Dan replied, "but there are no lights on in any of the cottages across the way. I'd say it's really late, maybe two or three o'clock. Let's follow him."

"In the *Polly Ann*?" Pete asked.

"No," Dan whispered, sliding out of his sleeping bag. "In Eddie's canoe. Come on."

Pete followed Dan, stacking up lots of good reasons why they shouldn't be doing what Dan was suggesting. Dan stepped over from the *Polly Ann* to the dock and nudged Eddie's sleeping bag.

"Eddie," Dan whispered. Eddie had evidently been awakened often by his summer neighbor. He didn't even hesitate as he threw open his sleeping bag and followed Dan and Pete through the boathouse door.

73

They ran along the dock to the green canoe. Eddie flipped the narrow craft into the water, and Dan hopped in the bow. Next, Pete stepped into the middle as Eddie grabbed a paddle and shoved off into the channel.

The stars glistened on the still water. In the distance, they saw the faint glimmering of tiny waves. The canoe in front of them was crossing the channel from Islington Point over toward the Elliot pier on LaSalle Island. The lead boat didn't stop there but continued **underneath** the Elliot dock. The three boys followed in amazement as the sides of their canoe skimmed the rocks between the fourth and fifth cribs of the hotel pier. They continued silently past two small boathouses in Elliot Row. The moon suddenly disappeared behind a fast-flying, cumulus cloud. Visibility dropped to zero.

"Hold it, Eddie," Dan whispered. "I can't see a thing."

Eddie set his paddle across his knees and the canoe drifted to a stop. A minute later, the moon again broke through the clouds; but the other boat had disappeared.

"Lost him," Dan groaned. He scanned the horizon. "You know this area pretty well, Pete. Where could he have gone?"

"Any number of places," Pete sighed in relief. He pointed along the shoreline. "The Davis boathouse here, the Long boathouse there. Mr. Geetings' island is just off to our right. He could be going to Urie Bay or Bosely Channel. One thing's for sure, he can make that canoe fly. He's probably a mile away by now."

"I guess so," Eddie agreed. "A good canoe can move pretty fast, and Joseph Red Owl's is as good a canoe as any in the Snows."

"Well," Pete said, "if he's going to either the Davis or the Long boathouse to steal food, he's going to be very disappointed. Doctor Davis wouldn't even keep minnow bait in his. And the Long boathouse has been empty for ten years—except for bats."

"Everyone knows Mr. Geetings' cabin's been cleared out and boarded up tight by the police. He won't be going there," Eddie said. "He must be heading for Urie Bay."

"There are no other boathouses until you get all the way to Preston's in Bosely Channel," Dan added. "I don't think the burglar would loot the same place twice in one week."

Another cloud moved across the moon's edge.

"Looks like the weather's closing back in," Dan said.

"Not much we can do now," Eddie sighed. "We might as well go home. Let's hope he comes back past our boathouse. We could follow him to his hideout."

"That is, if he returns at all," Dan said. "If it's Joseph Red Owl, he could be staying anywhere. He may have just gone in that reed bed yesterday to keep us from seeing where he really is camping."

"All right," Eddie agreed. "I don't know if I'll be able to get any sleep, but I'm sure going to give it a try."

The three retraced their route to Cincinnati Row and beached the canoe in front of Eddie's cottage. They stepped quietly into the boathouse and slipped into their sleeping bags. Eddie was snoring in less than a minute. Pete and Dan sat on the stern of the *Polly Ann* watching for the canoe to return along the channel. Eventually, though, exhaustion won out over curiosity and the two slid down onto the *Polly Ann*'s floor and fell asleep.

———

The sun was high the next morning before any of the three so much as budged from their sleeping bags.

Pete didn't even know he had a boathouse.

CHAPTER 13
BREAKFAST

Thursday, July 3 9:30 a.m.

"Getting you three to move this morning was like trying to raise the dead," Duke said, cutting a bite of Eggs Benedict. "I nearly had to set a charge under you to get you up for breakfast."

"Yeah," Neal growled at Eddie. Neal had practically an entire meal poised on his fork as he spoke. "Someone stepped on my foot and woke me up. What were you doing rumbling around in the boathouse at three a.m.?" He turned and glowered at Kate. "Hey, is the cherry blintz tray nailed to your end of the table, or what?"

"No, Neal," Kate replied sweetly. "All you need to do is ask politely. I'd be more than happy to pass it."

"Tell me, Neal," Stella added. "What did you do with all the money your parents gave you for your private etiquette lessons?"

Peggy followed immediately. "Oh, didn't you know? Neal is the star pupil at Ignoramus Institute. He has the highest annoyance quotient of anyone there. He nearly started World War III as a term project."

"Hey," Neal said, bristling, "you girls must have been pretty bored around here without me to pick on." He turned back to Dan. "So, what were you guys doing in the middle of the night, sleepwalking?" He glanced back at the girls, "Kate, are you going to send those blintzes down here, or do I have to come get 'em myself?"

From the other angle, Dan responded, "Pete woke me up when he saw a canoe going by on the other side of the channel. We thought it might be the boathouse burglar, so I got Eddie and the three of us went after him. We lost sight of him on the other side of the Elliot dock when the moon went behind a cloud."

"Did you get a look at who it was?" Ann asked, cutting a small wedge of cantaloupe with her knife and fork.

"Yeah, it was General MacArthur," Neal butted in.

"What is with you, Neal?" Peggy spun around and glared at her white-haired companion. "Does it bother you so much that you weren't included with the other guys that you've got to horn in on everything anyone says?"

"Oh, excuse me, Princess Margaret," Neal said, reaching across the table and grabbing the blintz tray. "No, that's not it. You think I'd want to go running around in the middle of the night chasing a two-bit crook with a bunch of losers? Not likely. Look, when you three are quite finished, I'm taking the *White Cap* and leaving. If you want a ride, you'd better hurry. I don't need to wait around here to be called an ignoramus. I can get that kind of treatment at home."

"Oh, come on, Neal," John Williams laughed. "There's no need to take this personally. Let's change the subject." He looked around the table. "All right, now," he smiled, "tomorrow night's the big Fourth of July party at Sand Bay. Does everyone have a date?"

For trying to lighten the conversation, John sure stirred up a hornets nest. One by one, each of the guests told who he or she was going with to the gala occasion. It came down to three people—Neal, Kate, and Pete. There was an awkward silence as Neal looked from face to face. Kate kept her eyes on Pete.

"I suppose _Peter_, here, has already asked you to the party," Neal said, interpreting Kate's stare. "Man, I take two weeks off to go to a basketball shooting camp with the Cincinnati Royals, I get personal coaching from Craig Dill—CRAIG DILL, mind you—he's the hottest rookie in the N.B.A., for you imbeciles, plus, I'm the top scorer in the camp. North Carolina, Michigan State, Indiana—practically every college coach in the nation wants me to visit his campus. Then I come up here just in time for open season on star athletes. I'm not going to beat around the bush, Kate. Are you coming with me tomorrow night or not?"

"Oh, Neal," Kate said. "I know we've always gone to the Fourth of July party together, but until a few days ago, I wasn't sure you were even coming up this year. So, when Pete asked last week, I told him I'd go with him. You understand," Kate said, looking Neal squarely in the eye.

Pete watched dumbstruck from his seat as the drama unfolded. He glanced at Kate in amazement. Until last night, Pete hadn't even heard about the Fourth of July party. And he'd certainly not been invited by anyone, let alone the most incredible girl in the Les Cheneaux Islands.

"Fine," Neal said as he shot a sharp look in Pete's direction. He bolted from his chair and strode to the front door. "Listen, I'm taking the *White Cap* and heading out. If anyone wants a ride home, they'd better get aboard. Now!" He held the knob, expecting everyone to jump.

"Well, I probably should be getting home early," Jane Blair said, wiping the corners of her mouth with a linen napkin. "House guests will be arriving from London this afternoon."

"And I could prepare for my riding lesson," Stella Moore said as she slid her chair away from the table.

Duke slowly uncorked himself to his full six-foot, five-inch stance and looked from Neal over to Eddie. "So, did you get a look at the guy?"

"Please?" Eddie inquired casually.

"The man you chased last night. Did you see him?"

"You mean the man in the canoe?" Eddie asked.

"Yes," Duke replied. "What did he look like?" Duke leaned against the table as if nothing Neal had said had even entered his mind.

"No," Eddie said. "He sure could handle a canoe, though."

"He went THROUGH the Elliot dock," Dan emphasized.

Kate stood and moved behind Pete's chair. She reached up and massaged Pete's shoulders. Pete instantly flushed and tried desperately to think of something to say that would show that he wasn't riled by Neal's antics, either.

"I've spent every summer of my life on that end of the island," Pete said slowly, "and I've never seen anyone do that. Day or night. I didn't know you could take a boat of any kind directly through the Elliot Hotel dock. Whoever it was knows this area like it's his own back yard."

Neal stared from the doorway, seething with rage. A moment passed. Everyone glanced from one to another, ignoring Neal as best he could.

"I'm out of here," Neal mumbled. He shoved the screen door open and charged down the stairs to the dock.

Neal's passengers, Duke, Stella, and Jane—the Marquette Island crowd—slowly made appropriate farewells to their hosts and started along the path to the shore. By the time they'd reached the red, double boathouse, however, the stern of the *White Cap* was disappearing around Islington Point and heading into Urie Bay.

"I don't know if my cottage is up to all that."

CHAPTER 14
ELLIOT ROW POTLUCK PLANS

Thursday, July 3 10:00 a.m.

"I'll take you three home," Dan said. "Everyone hop in my outboard."

The stranded Marquette Islanders moved down the dock to Dan's red and white Lyman. They all had summer homes on Club Point almost to Hessel.

"Good-bye," Kate waved to Dan's passengers as he started the Evinrude.

The outboard plowed away from the red, double boathouse. Gaining speed, the bow flattened down and the roostertail lengthened behind it as Dan steered a course past the Islington dock. From there, he took a bead on Connors Point. He slowed as he steered his way through a fleet of fishing boats and then turned north. At the end of Snows Channel, he brought his boat up to the wide Les Cheneaux Club dock. His three passengers hopped ashore and made their way along the trail to their summer homes.

Meanwhile, back at the red, double boathouse, Pete, Kate, and Eddie stood watching Dan's boat disappear in the distance. Pete looked over to Kate and Eddie. "Has Neal always been like that?" he asked.

"No, not at all," Kate reflected. "Until about three summers ago he was just a normal kid, very nice, really. Then, one night, we were at the Les Cheneaux Yacht Club for a party. Neal made an outlandishly rude comment about someone. His older brother, Don, who was home from college, heard him. Don laughed and said how much he was becoming like one of his older fraternity brothers. Well, that did it. Somehow Neal equated 'boorish' with 'suave,' and he's been trying to 'out-suave' himself ever since."

"I wonder if Neal's heart pumps with four chambers," Pete said. "I learned in science that snakes only have three."

"He's really not that bad a guy, once you get to know him," Eddie laughed. "It's just his misguided way of making friends."

"He must be trying to keep it to a pretty select few," Pete observed. "I've never met anyone like him. He sure isn't like any of your other friends."

"No, he's unique, all right," Eddie admitted. "Just don't let him get to you. Most of us pretend his comments go right over our heads. By now he must think we're all from the shallow end of the gene pool. My guess is, since he just arrived this week, he's giving us all another chance to prove we're worthy of associating with him. Also, for anyone new, like you, he wants to make sure you understand how incredibly brilliant he is and how biting his wit can be."

"Enough of Neal," Kate said. "What did you guys really find out last night?"

"Not much more than we told you," Eddie replied.

"Suppose the man you were following was the burglar," Kate said. "We don't know whether he was coming from or going to a break-in, do we? But if we go to the township office this afternoon, Mrs. Schoolcraft could tell us if there was a burglary last night. If there was, knowing where it was would tell us the route the man was taking when you saw him, wouldn't it?"

"That's right," Eddie said, his eyes wide open.

"Look," Pete said. "What if the guy we saw had nothing to do with it at all?"

"Yes, that's true," Kate admitted. "Well, we'll just have to go into town and check it out."

"I'll tell you what," Eddie yawned. "That was a long night. I'm ready for a snooze."

"Me, too," Pete agreed. "I'm dead on my feet. Before I go, though, there's something that's been bothering me. The other day we were talking about having the potluck at my place next week. I've been thinking. That was a pretty fancy affair last night. And the breakfast this morning? I don't know if my cottage is up to all that."

"Sure, it is," Eddie replied quickly. "We grilled the steaks ourselves on shore. We could do the same on your beach. I could bring the iron grate, if you don't have one. Look, it's not how fancy it is. It's the friends. Besides, each of us will bring a dish to pass, so that's no problem."

"Those steaks had to be pretty expensive," Pete added. "I've never even heard of filet mignon before. I doubt I could get my dad to pop for anything like that."

"We could have fish," Kate suggested. "It wouldn't take but about three of those big pike you keep showing off every day to feed the whole group. That would

83

be a real treat. We've never had fresh fish for a pot-luck."

"I don't know if we can cook fish on the beach," Pete said.

"Okay, we'll make an exception this time and have the dinner inside your cottage," Eddie said. "If that's okay with your parents."

"Oh, I don't think my parents would mind that," Pete said.

"Well, then, where's the rub?" Dan asked.

"First, there's the little matter of five girls squeez-ing into one double bunk bed," Pete went on. "You've seen my room. It's pretty small. And what about the breakfast? Until today, I'd never even seen a cherry blintz. And Eggs Benedict? I thought you were talking about what they asked Mr. Arnold on the morning of his execution—'Eggs, Benedict?'"

"Okay," Dan laughed, "how about this? We have the full group for potluck in your cottage, Pete. Then we have the campfire party on your beach. After that, the boys stay and sack out on shore or in your boat-house. The girls would take a boat back to Cincinnati Row for their sleepover. The next morning they could host the breakfast."

"It would be different, but it would work," Kate smiled. "What do you say, Pete?"

"Okay, I guess," Pete said, shrugging his shoulders. "I'll have to ask my mom and dad. I might need your help again to explain it. Would you mind? This time we'll ask them when my sister's not around. Hey, wouldn't that be something?—Neal and Cara for an evening's entertainment?"

"I think, by then, I'd have seen all the fireworks I'd want for one year," Eddie laughed.

"I bet you guys are tired," Kate said, "after your all-night chase."

"Yeah, I'm bushed," Pete admitted. "I'll meet you down here at three o'clock to go into town, okay?"

"Right," Eddie agreed as he turned toward shore. "See you then, Pete."

Kate followed Pete to the *Tiny Tin*. "Pete," she said as he loosened the bow line, "I hope you're not angry with me."

He turned in surprise. "What for?"

"For me telling Neal that you had already asked me to tomorrow's party," she said, taking a hold of Pete's hand. "I could see what was coming, and I was afraid I'd be stuck in my old role of having to be Neal's date. I really wanted to be with you. Every summer for years, he and I have gone to these things together." Kate's right hand tightened on Pete's left as she looked into his eyes. "So, will you be my date?" she asked with a smile.

"S-sure," Pete gulped. "That'd be great."

"Can you be here at six tomorrow night?"

"You bet," Pete said, stepping lightly into the *Tiny Tin*.

"And you won't forget about going into town with us this afternoon?" she added.

"I'll be here," Pete said, and he yanked the starting cord.

"Let's get a fill at Tassier's."

CHAPTER 15
PIERRE LeSOEUR

Thursday, July 3 11:00 a.m.

Pete went back to his cottage and crashed. He slept in his bunk until two that afternoon when the sun began to burn through the wavy glass window panes onto his face. He got up and found his mom and dad reading in their front porch rocking chairs. The sky was deep blue with an occasional puffy, white cloud drifting above the tall, green cedars. Sea gulls screeched along the shore, and crows cawed overhead.

"How was the potluck, Pete?" Averill Jenkins asked, looking up from her book.

"It was great. You wouldn't have believed the steak."

"You must have stayed up pretty late," Howard said.

"Yeah. Dan, Eddie, and I went for a little canoe ride. We didn't get a whole lot of sleep. Well, I told them I'd meet them at three to go into town. I'll be back by six."

Pete laced up his shoes and ran down the stone steps to the Elliot Row path. His sister had taken the *Tiny Tin*, so he decided to walk to Kate and Dan's. In ten minutes, he had passed the hotel, ducked through the bramble tunnel, and trotted the mile along Cincinnati Row to the Hinken's cottage. He found his three friends stretched out on beach towels wearing swim suits. They slipped into some sandals and tee-shirts and hopped aboard Dan's boat. In minutes, they were in town standing before Mrs. Schoolcraft in the Clark Township office.

———

"Horsburgh's?" Kate asked in astonishment. "On Coryell? That makes no sense at all."

"Well," Betty Schoolcraft said, looking at the sheet before her, "that's who turned in a complaint this morning. About ten o'clock. West side of Coryell right across from Island Number Eight. Mr. Horsburgh came in himself. His list was just like the others—food, beer, pop, potato chips . . ."

"Still no idea who's doing it?" Dan asked.

"Not a clue," Mrs. Schoolcraft replied.

"Come on, guys," Kate said. "Let's talk about this over a Jersey Mud."

The four walked along Hodeck Street until Eddie opened the door to the Bon Air. The place was packed, but they found a table by the jukebox and sat down.

"How could that guy you saw in the canoe last night have gotten from the west side of LaSalle Island to the west side of Coryell?" Kate asked.

"And what was he doing by the Islington Hotel?" Eddie continued. "I wonder if it might be one of those other men that Mrs. Schoolcraft told us about—Pierre What's-his-name or that Mickey guy."

"Didn't she say Pierre was camping on Bass Cove Lake?" Dan asked. "That's a pretty remote area, but it's not very far from Coryell if you cut around Government Island."

"Well," Kate said. "Let's go look in on him."

"Right now?" Pete asked.

"Sure, right now," Dan said, pushing his chair back.

"Bass Cove is a couple hour walk from my place," Pete argued. "And the trail is miserable. Mosquitoes, snakes, swamp . . ."

"So, we go by boat," Kate said. "If you take Bosely Channel into Lake Huron and follow the shore to the east, you can see Bass Cove Lake from the water."

"I've never gone that way," Pete admitted. "My parents made me promise never to go out onto Lake Huron alone."

"You won't be alone," Dan smiled. "We'll be with you. Honestly, Pete, sometimes I wonder if you understand parents at all. Don't you see? It's called reverse psychology. As a parent, one of their jobs is to get us to do things, you know, have experiences. They think we won't want to do them if they just say, `Go do this,' so they tell us, `Don't do this.' So, naturally, we do them. All the stuff your parents have been telling you not to do, they really want you to do. They get points for each of our activities. Right now, I'd be willing to bet your parents are failing the course. On the other hand, when Kate and I graduate from high school, our parents will have the most points in the country. They'll be so proud. Really! Quit laughing. I'm not making this up."

"Besides," Kate grinned as she took Pete's hand, "Bass Cove is right along the shore. It's not like it's across on the other side of Lake Huron or anything."

"Come on," Eddie said, "we'll take Dan's outboard. When we get close to the beach, I'll row in to shore."

"What about the Jersey Mud?" Pete asked, stalling for time.

"Later," Dan said. "I'll treat."

"Okay, what are we waiting for?" Kate said.

Pete could think of several things. Standing face to face with Pierre LeSoeur leaped to the top of the list. "What if he really is doing all the break-ins?" Pete asked. "I doubt if he's going to be real neighborly to four kids stumbling onto his secret hideout."

"Only way to know is to go," Dan replied. He stood up and headed for the door. Pete brought up the rear, Kate tugging him along.

In minutes, they were heading out of Cedarville harbor in Dan's boat.

"Check the gas, Eddie," Dan yelled up to the bow.

Eddie lifted the fuel tank under the bow seat. "She's kind of low," Eddie yelled back. "Let's get a fill at Tassier's. I've got a couple bucks."

Dan pulled into the gas dock and hopped out carrying the can. Leo Tassier was just coming out of the oil shed.

"What'll it be, kids."

"Gas and oil, Mr. Tassier," Dan replied, handing the can to the Shell station owner. "Say, have you seen Joseph Red Owl around?"

"Lots of people been looking for him lately," Leo said as he poured a half a pint of oil into the tank. He turned to the gas pump. "Yeah, I saw him a couple of days ago in his canoe. He was coming out from down there by Taylor Lumber," he nodded back toward town. "He went by me here and headed along the shore toward Islington Point. Haven't seen him since, though." He lifted the nozzle from the can. "That'll be a buck seventy for the gas and thirty cents for the oil."

"Thanks, Mr. Tassier," Eddie said, handing him two singles.

"What about Pierre LeSoeur?" Kate pressed. "Have you seen him?"

"Nope," Leo Tassier answered. "Can't say as I have. Not lately, anyhow. He stays about as far away from town as he can. Most folks are glad of that. Me, for one. He's a real rough character. It's like someone snatched him out of a cave and dropped him here to test civilized folk."

"And this Mickey O'Flynn guy?" Kate asked. "What about him?"

"Dick Dice, he pumps gas for me on the weekends, he told me this morning that he saw Mickey crossing Scammons Harbor toward Hill Island, dragging a line behind his canoe. He could be roughing it on Government. Now, there's someone no one should cross. I saw him carve up a man in a bar one time for no reason at all. You're not asking so you can go snooping on these degenerates, are you? Because if you are, you'd very quickly wish you hadn't."

"No, nothing like that," Dan said. "It's just that our boathouse was broken into the other night, and we heard Sheriff Shoberg was asking about them. We thought if we could get some information, it might help him catch whoever's doing it. Well, is everybody set? Let's head out."

———

"We're not still going to Bass Cove, are we?" Pete yelled to Dan over the high-pitched whine of the Evinrude.

"We won't land or anything, Pete. I promise," Dan yelled back as they skimmed past Islington Point. "We'll just look around from a ways out."

90

Dan slowed as he approached the narrow entrance to Bosely Channel. He cut the throttle almost to STOP and kept to the right, staying near the deeper shore-line. The motor echoed softly in the windless passage and then resonated deeply as they cruised in front of a large, three-well boathouse. In the last stall, the *White Cap* sat motionless, tethered to four posts.

"Is that Neal's dock?" Pete asked, recognizing the mahogany speedboat. Pete had gone through Bosely Channel hundreds of times never thinking much about the impressive boathouse. To him, it was just some rich person's property.

"Yes, and that's the road to his place," Dan explained, pointing to a narrow, dirt path that cut sharply into the forest.

Neal's got a ROAD to his cottage? Pete thought. *Holy Cow! It must be a mansion.*

"Their summer home looks out over Lake Huron about a mile away," Dan added. "They keep their boats here to protect them from the heavy swells of the big lake."

They continued to the end of the mile-long cut and slowed to a crawl where Bosely Channel widens and becomes almost too shallow to navigate. Dan tilted his motor for the last ten yards to keep the prop from hitting bottom. It didn't seem possible that only four days ago, right here, the black-hulled speedboat had exploded, killing Fats.

Once into Lake Huron, Dan nudged the throttle up a notch and headed east along the LaSalle Island shore. They watched for boulders along the rocky coast and finally came around a point and entered Bass Cove Bay. From there it was easy to see Bass Cove Lake just in-land from the Lake Huron shoreline.

Dan cut the engine and tilted the prop as Eddie put oars in the oarlocks. Eddie made several strokes with his back to the shore before Kate nudged him. "Hold it, Eddie," she whispered. "There he is."

"<u>Arretez!</u> Come no closer!" a rough-looking man wearing a black coat and red sash yelled out from shore. He cocked his double-barreled shotgun and held it high. "Perhaps you are here for more of what I gave your smart-mouthed, white-haired friend this morning?"

Dan turned to Eddie and whispered, "Neal Preston. Pierre must have shot at him this morning. I bet he thinks Neal sent us."

"Whatever Neal got, he probably had coming," Eddie replied. "I can only imagine what he said to rile the old trapper."

Dan called back to the man on shore, "We've just come to fish. We hear there's some pretty big pike in there."

"No, <u>messieurs</u>, no fish at all. Leave now or I shoot."

"He's got us surrounded, Dan," Pete whispered frantically. "Let's get out of here. Whatever it was he gave Neal, you can bet none of us would want even some of."

"Okay, mister," Dan called out sitting down.

Eddie spun the boat around and rowed away from shore. Farther out, Dan let the prop down and pulled the starter cord. He steered around the southern point of LaSalle Island and back toward Bosely Channel. He checked the throttle to SLOW and entered the shallow pass.

"Let's have a talk with Neal," Kate said anxiously. "I've got to find out what happened this morning."

"We'll call him on the intercom from his boat-house," Dan agreed. "We're almost there."

"Neal, we're at your dock."

CHAPTER 16
THE CONFRONTATION

Thursday, July 3 5:15 p.m.

"Neal," Eddie said into the boathouse phone, "we're at your dock. We'd like to talk to you. Dan, Kate, Pete, and I just saw Pierre LeSoeur at Bass Cove. . . . Yes, he seemed <u>plenty</u> annoyed. . . . Okay, we'll wait." Eddie cradled the receiver and turned to his friends. "He'll be right down."

In five minutes, a 1930, Ford Woody station wagon rattled along the narrow lane out from the woods and pulled to a stop next to the boathouse. Neal hopped out of the driver's seat and ambled over to his four visitors.

"Was that you the old Frenchman was talking about?" Eddie asked.

"What do you mean?" Neal replied to Eddie. He nodded coldly to Kate and Dan ignoring Pete completely.

"We just about got shot over in Bass Cove," Dan said. "We went there to take a look around. Before we'd even come within thirty yards of shore, Pierre

93

LeSoeur boiled out of his shack with his muzzle-loader and told us to scram. Something he said made us think you'd spoken with him this morning. Is that right?"

"Yeah, well, I paid him a little visit," Neal said, cocking his head. "I told him that my boathouse had been broken into the other night and that I was looking for what was stolen. I said that I wanted to check his cabin. He made a suggestion as to where I might look instead, and I told him where he could stick his suggestion. All of a sudden, he pulls this blunderbuss out from behind him and tells me to get off his property. I reminded him that we were on public land, and I had as much right to be there as he did. Boy, that got him. He jammed the barrel against my nose and cocked the thing. I took his advice and got back in my boat. I rowed about twenty yards before I yelled out to him what I'd do when I came back. He aimed and put a load of buckshot right over my head—like to deafen me for life. It was a while before the echo died down, but I could tell he wasn't finished; his lips were still moving—big. I told him he'd have to repeat himself, that I hadn't heard him; he about came unglued. He said that next time, he'd have ol' *Antoinette* sighted in a little better. He's a feisty one, he is. I'll get him, though. He'll learn not to mess with a Cincinnati Preston."

"That wasn't very bright, Neal," Kate said. "What possessed you to tell him right out that you thought he was the burglar?"

"I'm a man of few words, Kate," Neal said, leaning smugly against the car. "I say what I mean, and I mean what I say. Besides, why should you three have all the fun playing cops and robbers? I decided to do a little detective work myself."

94

"You're a nitwit," Eddie said. "You could have been killed out there. And just a suggestion. You might start your conversations with a smile instead of a left hook. A lot of people take offense to that. Besides, you'll make life a lot easier for the rest of us."

"All right," Neal retorted, "so I was a little abrupt. I figured there wasn't any sense mincing words with him. I hate it when people waste my time, . . . like you're doing right now. Suppose you tell me what you know about this boathouse deal."

"Look, Neal," Dan said evenly, "all we're doing is helping Sheriff Shoberg. If we find something, we're going straight to him with it. From what we hear about the people he's watching, you should probably do the same, especially with your track record in public relations."

Neal stared from Dan to Eddie to Kate with a look of arrogant disdain. He turned, hopped in the Woody, and headed back along the dirt road kicking up a cloud of dust.

"I've got a hunch Neal's going to get us into some real trouble," Dan said as he led the other three to his boat.

That stopped Pete in his tracks. In the few weeks Pete had known Dan, he'd learned that Dan's hunches were as good as fish in a frying pan. He hoped, for once, Dan would be wrong.

"The parents went in the Williams' Sea Wolf."

CHAPTER 17
FIREWORKS

Friday July, 4 6:00 p.m.

"Oh, Pete," Kate said as the *Tiny Tin* approached the red, double boathouse, "I'm so glad you could come."

"Where is everyone?" Pete asked, handing her the bow line.

"Dan and Eddie took the *Silver Moon* about an hour ago to tow a pontoon raft to Sand Bay. It's very shallow over there, so they'll use it to help everyone ashore. Our parents went with the Williams in the *Sea Wolf*. You and I will go in the *Polly Ann*." She turned and faced Pete, his eyes were cast down. "What's the matter, Pete? Is something wrong?"

"No, but before I left I told my mom and dad about us going to Bass Cove yesterday and seeing Pierre. I'll tell you what, they're not real happy about this boathouse mystery. I'm really lucky they let me come to the party tonight."

"Well, I'm glad they did," Kate said. She clasped Pete's hand as he stepped onto the dock. Her soft hair brushed his cheek; she smelled like fresh lilacs.

They walked inside the boathouse and boarded the old Hacker-Craft. Kate pressed the starter and a low rumble echoed throughout the building. She backed the *Polly Ann* slowly out of the slip, turned into the channel, and pushed the throttle ahead. The *Polly Ann* cut majestically through the dark blue water of Elliot Bay. Kate steered her toward Connors Point, through Middle Entrance, and into Lake Huron. She followed the white markers back along the south shore of Little LaSalle Island to Sand Bay. There, perhaps thirty mahogany speedboats were anchored a few yards off shore. Several camp fires, volleyball nets, and over a hundred people of all ages lined the beach. The party was just getting under way.

As the *Polly Ann* approached, Dan and Eddie poled the pontoon raft out to meet them. Pete dropped anchor and joined Kate on the wide, flat-decked boat.

Pete scanned the crowd. Off to the left, he saw Neal Preston standing near a bonfire talking to a girl. Pete followed as Kate jumped ashore. They moved toward a group of people on the right.

Pete looked around. What a layout! It must have taken a company of men to bring all the equipment to this uninhabited part of Little LaSalle Island. An entire bandstand and dance floor were set up along the beach. There were picnic tables, awnings, Venetian lamps, flags, red, white, and blue bunting—everything.

"How do you want your steak, Pete," Eddie asked, coming up from behind. "Chef Beau from the Grand Hotel is taking orders."

"You're kidding," Pete said. "The Grand Hotel on Mackinac Island?"

"Sure," Eddie replied. "He and a staff of waiters come every year. See those men over there in the tuxedos?

97

That's the dance band from Chicago. They'll be starting after dinner and playing until after midnight. When it's dark we'll have fireworks set off from the pontoon boat in the middle of the bay. So, how do you want your steak?"

"Medium, I guess," Pete said remembering the potluck two nights before.

"Medium it is then," Eddie said and went over to the barbecue area.

Pete and Kate spread a beach blanket and sat with several of the potluck crowd.

———

The sun was down and night had set in by the time Pete and Kate finished their steaks and corn-on-the-cob. Kate hopped up, took Pete by the hand, and the two moved out onto the dance floor. The band played "Glow Worm" and "Unforgettable" before the conductor signaled the end of the set. Pete and Kate swayed for a moment after the music had stopped. They looked into each others' eyes and turned from the dance floor. They followed an old, logging road into the woods. A tall platform of cedar planks formed a shelter a few yards from the beach. It looked like an ancient Indian gathering place, a prehistoric temple.

Kate leaned against a corner post and took both of Pete's hands in hers. She looked out into the bay and up at the dazzling canopy of brilliant stars that glowed overhead. She closed her eyes gently drawing Pete toward her. Pete had never kissed a girl, except for the obligatory pecks at the cheeks of his sisters and cousins, so this was pretty new to him. He was more than willing to break some ground here, but he had no idea how willing until she brushed her soft, warm lips against his. It nearly made his eyes cross.

Instantly, bolts of lightening flashed throughout the heavens.

Thunder rocked Pete's soul as well as the entire Sand Bay sky.

He opened his eyes half expecting to be snatched up into the hereafter. He'd go willingly now, there being nothing left to live for.

Missiles whistled overhead. Gigantic formations of colored stardust shot across the heavens. Red, white, and blue flumes exploded all around the bay. The Milky Way paled to the grandeur of the fireworks in and around Pete's head.

———

Pete put one arm around Kate's waist and they walked back toward the party. The band from Chicago played, and the chef from the Grand Hotel created extravagant desserts. As other people danced, talked, and sang, Pete and Kate walked along the beach barely leaving footprints in the soft sand.

"Let's take the girls sailing."

CHAPTER 18
THE CHALLENGE

Saturday, July 5   4:00 p.m.

"We've been challenged to a basketball game with the Cedarville guys," Duke repeated over the din of the Bon Air crowd. "They still can't believe we beat them at softball, so now they want to take us on in hoops. Ten of them have been practicing every day for the last week up at the high school gym."

"How good are you at roundball, Pete?" Dan asked.

"Depends on who's guarding me," Pete smiled. "But I did make the school team this year."

Dan looked at Duke. "Have you asked Neal?" Dan asked.

"Yes," Duke answered. "He said he'd lend his talents if the mood struck him. I'll tell you what, if he's half as good as he says, the rest of us can stay home."

"When's the game?" Eddie asked.

"Tuesday. Seven thirty," Duke replied. "The Les Cheneaux Rotary Club is putting it on. A kid from Hessel's in the hospital with polio. They're raising money to pay for an iron lung. Unless they can get him one soon, Doc Blue says he won't live through the summer. My dad's Rotary Club in Cincinnati has agreed to match funds. The Snows' Rotarians have reserved the gym and plan on charging a buck a head for admission," Duke added. "They're hoping that, because we beat the Cedarville guys at softball, every man, woman, and child in Mackinac County will want to be there—like it's a big, Western showdown."

"Tuesday," Dan said. "This Tuesday?"

"That's right," Duke nodded. "Seven thirty."

"Three days. That's not much time," Dan shook his head. "Can we get the gym for a practice?"

"Yes," Duke replied. "Monday afternoon for two hours. I've told everyone except you three. Where've you been?"

"Oh, just trying to figure out the boathouse burglaries," Eddie said.

"Have you found anything new?" Duke asked.

"No," Eddie answered. "Nothing for sure, anyway."

"Well, practice is at three o'clock Monday at the high school. Can you be there?"

"Sure," Dan said for everyone, "count us in."

————

Monday, July 7 3:00 p.m. Cedarville High School

"We must be nuts to be in here," a college-aged guy yelled to a friend across the gym floor. "We should be out sailing."

"Yes, this is insane," the other replied. "It's got to be a hundred and ten in here."

"And that's just the humidity," someone else quipped.

"I'm out of here," another said. "Let's take the girls swimming. Basketball's not my sport, anyway. Hey, Moose, Duke, you guys coming?"

"I'm sticking around awhile," Moose Harding said.

"Me, too," Duke Armour agreed.

Pete glanced through the gym at the five remaining players.

"I guess we're it," Eddie said as the door closed behind the last of the escapees. "All the sane people are gone."

And he was right. This was not a day that anyone with two working brain cells would be caught running around in an airtight, glass-enclosed building. Whoever had decided on basketball for a grudge match certainly had never played indoors in July. So now, it was down to Pete, Eddie, Dan, Duke, and Moose.

And

then,

Neal

strolled

in.

His blondish-white hair and pink complexion practically lit up the darkened gym. He wore snow white, high-top Converse All-Star basketball shoes, gold knee pads, and a brilliant red satin uniform with a gold number 4 on the front and back. He was a sight.

"Where is everyone?" he asked as he bounced his brand new leather ball on the wooden floor. The thump echoed throughout the otherwise silent gymnasium.

"We're all that's left," Eddie answered. "I hope you're here to play."

"You'd better believe it," Neal said with a swagger both in his step and his voice. "I'm your point guard."

"We kind of had Pete pencilled in for that," Duke said.

Neal stopped in his tracks. "Didn't I tell you where I've been for the past two weeks? Or maybe you've

102

forgotten. To remind you, I was at the Cincinnati Royals shooting camp on the U.C. campus. That's the <u>N.B.A</u> Cincinnati Royals. Craig Dill and I have been trading basketball tips. Craig Dill, mind you—starting forward for the Royals? Now, who's playing point guard?" Neal smirked as he cocked his head.

Moose Harding, his muscled, six-foot four-inch frame sweating profusely, waited patiently for Neal to finish his presentation. He glanced casually at the other players. "Frankly," he drawled, "I don't think Neal's going to need us. Let's go for a swim." He turned and started for the door.

"Hold it," Duke said, grabbing Moose by the shirt. "Look. We can't back out now. We're going to need anyone who's willing to suit up."

Moose turned. "Even Loudmouth, here? You know, I'm not sure our gym shoes are high enough. We may need waders. Neal could turn this place into a skating rink in five . . ."

"Okay, okay," Duke interrupted. "Let's just play a little half-court, three-on-three to get an idea of who can do what."

"Fine," Neal said, jerking his nose in the air. "I'm willing. Let's see. How about Moose, Duke, and me against you three bigtime detectives?" Neal challenged. He stripped off his jersey exposing his well-muscled chest and arms and stared at Dan and Eddie.

"You'd better keep your shirt on, Neal," Eddie said. "Your chip is going to fall off your shoulder."

"Oh, yeah? Well, how about a little side bet here, Eddie?" Neal screamed, jumping into Eddie's face. "A hundred bucks says I can outscore you three losers all by myself."

"Another time, Neal," Eddie said. "Let's just play ball, okay?"

For the next ten minutes, to the astonishment of the others, Neal put on a shooting clinic hitting jumpers from all over the court. First, Dan tried to guard him, but Neal slipped past him easily and made shots from every possible angle. Then Pete defended him which seemed to inspire Neal to even greater heights of showmanship. Next, Eddie took a turn. It became obvious that Neal could outmaneuver any single person that tried to check him. Once the ball got into his hands, he invariably took the shot. What was remarkable, though, was that he never missed. Not once.

Eddie motioned for Dan and Pete to double-team Neal as soon as he got the ball. Immediately, the shooting show was over. Neal didn't have room to set himself for good shots, so he fired wildly at the hoop. He missed repeatedly but still refused to pass to Duke or Moose. Soon, it became evident that Neal not only couldn't play team offense, he couldn't play defense worth a lick, either.

The momentum quickly flowed to the other side. Eddie, Dan, and Pete, playing with less talent but with flawless teamwork, soon went ahead.

"Hey, cut this double-teaming stuff out!" Neal yelled. "You've got to give me some space."

Duke calmly picked up the ball and motioned everyone to gather under the basket. "Look, Neal, we're going to need your help tomorrow night," he began. "I'll be the first to admit, you're a great shooter, but you saw what happened when Pete and Dan double-teamed you. Imagine what the Cedarville guys will do to us playing full court, five-on-five. Unless you've been keeping your passing talents a secret for the last hour, the rest of us will never see the ball."

"Duke's right," Dan agreed. "They'll figure you out real quick. They'll plant one guy inside your shirt full time and have two others so close, your mother in the stands won't be able to find you. If we're going to have a chance, you've got to pass and help on defense. If you don't, it'll be all over by the end of the first quarter."

"Look," Pete said to the other four. "I'll be glad to sit the whole game. Maybe Neal can pull it off. Maybe he is a one-man team."

"That won't happen, Pete, and you know it," Moose cut in. "We're going to need teamwork if we have any chance at all. We're already at a disadvantage with their having ten solid players and a week of practice."

"That's it, guys," a voice called from the other end of the gym. "I've got to lock up now." It was a man dressed in overalls holding an eight-foot gymnasium mop.

The six sweaty resorters slowly headed for the exit. Neal picked up the ball and flicked it toward the basket from half court. Swoosh. The bottom of the net snapped up through the top of the rim. The backspin on the ball brought it bouncing back like an obedient puppy, rolling to Neal's feet.

"You're unreal, Neal," Moose said. "You're the best shooter I've ever seen. Would it be too much to ask if you would just grow up between now and 7:30 tomorrow night?"

———

Tuesday, July 8 8:00 p.m.

The score stood sixteen to twelve in favor of the Resorters at the end of the first quarter. The packed gym

105

of three hundred fans had watched Neal run off fourteen straight points to start the game before the dazed Cedarville captain called a time-out. When they broke their huddle, to the surprise of everyone, the Cedarville defenders left Neal completely alone. When the ball came to him, however, three of their players closed in like leeches on a lake trout. Time after time, for the next five minutes, Neal would get the ball and then force a terrible shot. The Cedarville team stormed back on offense and took the lead early in the second quarter.

There were still two minutes left in the first half when Eddie came down with a rebound and crashed to the floor. "Time!" he screamed in agony. Three hundred people gasped as he rolled under the basket. Dan and Pete helped him to the bench, but it was clear that he was gone for the rest of the game. It would be five cottagers against the "Cedarville Ten" the rest of the way.

The first half ended with the score 30 to 24. The Cedarville All-Stars were on their way to a blow-out.

The second half started and life got progressively worse for the vacationers. Neal fired a barrage of bad shots at the offensive end and played defense about as seriously as a musky minding a minnow.

Duke called for a time-out. It was still early in the third quarter. Something dramatic had to be done. The five huddled on the sideline, Duke running the show.

"Pete, you're at the point," Duke said calmly. "Dan, you're on one wing. Moose, you and I will trade at high and low post."

"I'll take the other wing, right?" Neal said.

"Wrong, Neal," Duke said staring into his face. "You'll take a seat. We'll play with four players."

"You can't be serious!" Neal screamed.

106

"Watch me," Duke said, shoving his fist up under Neal's nose. "Sit down."

Neal stared blankly at Duke as he slumped onto the bench next to Eddie.

Pete took the point guard position and the game changed instantly. It was strange to watch, four against five, but suddenly the Resorters became effective. Maybe it was the adrenaline, but everything they did, worked. Pete fed Duke and Moose inside for easy buckets. He and Dan each popped a couple from the perimeter. Before long, the game was tied.

The vacationers took the floor to start the fourth quarter, still using only four players. Eddie sat in agony with a swollen ankle, and Neal sat next to him in an entirely different sort of anguish.

Cedarville, with a one-man advantage, sagged into a tight zone defense. The Resorters began to fade playing in the hot gym against a steady stream of fresh players. Cedarville ran off nine straight points, and the rout was on.

Duke called for another time-out with two minutes left in the game. His three teammates came to the sideline panting heavily around him. Duke stared down at Neal. "You think you can play team ball for two minutes?" Duke puffed. "If you can, we've still got a chance."

"Yeah," Neal said, his eyes cast to the floor. "Let me in."

The referee checked the ball and Dan inbounded it to Pete. The Cedarville players smiled and went back to their special "Neal" defense leaving him open until he got the ball. Pete saw him on the right wing and got it to him. As Neal eyed the hoop, three Cedarville players converged like sea gulls to fish guts. Neal made a head fake, and the three nearly jumped out of the gym. That left Moose and Pete wide open under the basket. Neal bounce-passed the ball to Moose who laid it up for two points.

Cedarville came back on a fast break, but Neal stripped the ball from their center and fired a strike to Duke at the other end for a lay-up. With one minute to go and the Resorters behind by three points, Neal made another steal and passed it to Dan who scored easily.

The Resorters trailed by only one point with twenty seconds remaining.

Cedarville inbounded and put on a stall to run out the clock, but Moose intercepted a weak pass and flipped it to Neal at center court. Five seconds on the clock. Neal glanced ahead. Pete had a clear shot four feet from the basket. Instead, Neal took one dribble, eyed the rim, and fired a high arcing shot almost to the rafters.

The buzzer sounded as the ball ripped toward the basket.

B-wang-ang-ang.

The ball caught on the front of the rim and caromed all the way back to center court.

———

The final score of the First Annual Rotary For Polio Basketball Game was Cedarville 67, The Resorters, 66.

The only important figure that was kept, however, was that the Les Cheneaux Rotary Club had collected $380 in donations from the community. An equal amount would arrive shortly from the Cincinnati Rotary Club. The total would be more than enough to give the Hessel boy a fighting chance in his battle against the life-threatening disease.

108

Mickey found a change purse in the red, double boathouse.

CHAPTER 19
THE STING

Tuesday, July 8 9:00 p.m.

After the game, at center court, Doctor Robert Scruton, head of the polio unit at Sault Sainte Marie Hospital, was presented the receipts from the basketball gate by Rotary President, Jack Geist. Jack, along with Coach Bill Ebinger, the game's organizer and referee, escorted Dr. Scruton into town. At the first lamp post on Hodeck Street, Bill and Jack shook hands with Dr. Scruton and left him to walk the last sixty feet to his car.

———

On the night that Mickey O'Flynn found the change purse in the red boathouse, he had gone straight to the Cedar Bar. He ordered a beer and overheard the bartender discussing a basketball game that a bunch of Cedarville men were getting ready to play. It would be held at the high school gym on the night of July the eighth and all the proceeds were to be given to some Hessel boy.

Mickey couldn't imagine that anyone needed money any more than he did. He decided right then that he was going to be the beneficiary of their noble gesture.

———

Out from the dark Mickey sneaked up to Dr. Scruton. He quickly tied and gagged the doctor and pushed him into a ditch alongside his car. He grabbed the thick envelope of money and dashed to the harbor. He boarded his canoe and lit out for Cedarville Channel. It was ten minutes before someone happened along and found Dr. Scruton crawling out of the muddy trench.

One of the Cedarville players, Bob Arfstrom, later told Sheriff Shoberg that he had seen someone racing across the street toward the bay, but, at the time, thought nothing of it. He was too busy thanking his stars that he had gotten away with the sloppy pass that almost cost his team the game. He could only say that, whoever it was, wasted no time in the street lights getting to the harbor.

*They brought Neal's boat
alongside the makeshift dock.*

CHAPTER 20
PETE'S POTLUCK

Wednesday, July 9 6:00 p.m.

Three boats were already tied to the Jenkins' long, rickety dock when the *White Cap* roared into Elliot Bay. Neal Preston throttled her down as he approached the shallow area. Duke held a bow line standing next to Neal; the two girls, Jane Blair and Stella Moore, sat in the stern. The nose of the powerful speedboat flattened into the green water twenty yards from the welcoming committee of potluck guests.

Neal had never come into this part of Elliot Bay and was unfamiliar with the water. He approached cautiously, knowing that a boulder could poke a hole in the *White Cap*'s hull and put a severe crimp in his summer. He inched forward and cut the engine coasting up to the dock. Duke tossed the bow line over Eddie's outstretched arm. John Williams took a stern line from Stella, and together they brought the speedboat alongside the two-plank wide, makeshift dock.

"This looks a little precarious," Neal said, standing in the boat. "I wouldn't want to try this on a stormy night."

"The water's up this year," Pete said, ignoring the slight. After all, it was true. The dock was shaky. "The ice is so bad along here that we have to rebuild the dock every summer."

"Mr. and Mrs. Jenkins have dinner about ready," Dan said. "Let's head up to the cottage. I can't wait to get into a few of those pike and bass Pete keeps showing off every day."

They made their way off the dock and up the winding stone steps to the Jenkins' cabin. Pete stepped ahead pulling open the screen door. There was barely space in the cramped living room for his ten guests to stand now that the center table had been opened and its three leaves inserted.

The setting was lovely. Two long candles in the middle of the table were lit, even though it wasn't yet dark. Most of the china plates matched, and real glass glasses were set out instead of the ordinary rubber ones. Everyone had his own paper napkin; and each place was set with a silver-plated knife, fork, and spoon—some with more silver than others.

Pete couldn't remember when so many people had come for dinner in his cottage. It looked like the old pictures he had seen when his mom was about his age and the cabin was new. Boy, they had parties then. All the men would be dressed in suits and tall hats; the women wore long, white dresses and wide-brimmed bonnets. Even the kids would be decked out like it was some sort of church social.

Pete glanced around wondering what the others thought of his cottage. Everyone was chattering about all the relics that hung on the bare wood walls between the two-by-fours. Kerosene lanterns, tin-type photographs, and crude carvings adorned the living room. The boys marvelled at the ancient fishing equipment and the wood-burning stove. The girls talked about the birch bark-framed picture of Hiawatha and Minnehaha, the sweet grass baskets, and the antique furniture. It was all so different, like a museum, so unbelievably old and quaint.

Pete followed their stares, listening as each object was discussed. This was all just ordinary stuff to him, things he and his family used every day. To his new friends, though, it was like some extravagant historic exhibit. He suddenly hoped none of them would need the services of a bathroom. "Cute and quaint" would turn to, "What? You're kidding? I'm not going in there!" when they made their trek back to the old, two-hole outhouse, home to many of the island's crickets and spiders. There was nothing cute and quaint about that, he was sure, although it suited him just fine, except in the middle of the night.

Mr. and Mrs. Jenkins began bringing in trays of fish from the kitchen. "Pete," Howard Jenkins called out, "you, Dan, and Eddie can help serve the other dishes. Everyone else may be seated."

Pete watched in dismay as Neal sat down next to Kate in the place he had planned for himself. Neal picked up a spoon and raised an eyebrow. It was the one spoon that had no silver left at all. Neal tilted his plate eyeing the crack down the middle and about an inch chip out of the edge. Then Neal inspected his drinking cup. Pete had set that for himself, too. It was the last one in the cottage, a green rubber one that Pete normally used anyway. It worked and everything, but it was hardly something you'd set in front of your biggest critic. The edge was rough, chewed on, like Pete's math pencils. He watched as Neal showed the cup to Kate. She frowned at him but the message was clear.

Pete plunged immediately from the sublime notion that he was hosting a terrific dinner party in one of the world's most interesting settings to the realization that he'd suckered some very important people into what might possibly be the most butt-ugly, ill-deserving dining place on earth. Neal had an innate talent for making a "Gift From God" seem like something you should scrape from your heels before coming in from a cow barn.

Pete's fears dissipated quickly, however, as the thick, golden fried filets made their way around the table. Everyone oohed and aahed until the platter got to Neal.

"These aren't from around here, are they?" Neal growled, evidently unaware of the Snows' world-wide reputation for fresh-water sportfishing. "My aunt says that the only fish that are safe to eat come from the North Atlantic. If you get them from the Great Lakes, they're all infested with worms. They swim around looking for hooks just to get out of the water."

Everyone looked down at their plates as though someone had waved a wand over the table and turned their entree into raw sewage.

"I don't know," Pete said, shrugging his shoulders. "I've been eating fish up here every summer day since I was five. I caught these myself and, believe me, they were plenty healthy this morning."

Everyone except Neal slowly resumed their meal, first with small bites, and then with a vengeance.

For several minutes, the only sounds were those of forks clanking and jaws chomping.

"Corn!" Neal thundered from his place across from Pete.

Everyone snapped their heads up and saw Neal scowling.

"I want the corn. Can't you see that no one's passed me the corn?"

Pete quickly grabbed the bowl that had stopped in front of him. As he began to send it across the table, Peggy intercepted it.

"You're not getting this or anything else until you ask politely," she said softly and with an angelic smile. "Sometimes, Neal, you can be the biggest embarrassment."

Just then Howard Jenkins came in from the kitchen with another heaping tray of fish still sizzling from the pan. He made room for the platter by sliding the corn over in front of Neal. Neal grabbed it and sneered at Peggy.

From the other end of the table Ann Early spoke up. "Honestly, Mr. Jenkins, this is the best potluck we've ever had. I've never eaten anything so good. Until I met Pete, I didn't know fish like this lived around here."

Eventually even Neal, hunger overcoming his obvious misgivings about the main course, began nibbling at, and then devouring three large filets. Howard Jenkins came in from the kitchen displaying two pies—one apple and one cherry. "I'm taking orders," he said. "Who wants which and with or without a la mode?"

———

Soon dinner was over and everyone pitched in and cleared the dishes. Pete scraped the leftovers onto three trays and set them out back near the kitchen window. Eddie poured boiling water in one side of the double sink and Dan carried cold water from the outside catch tank to cool it down. Eddie and Dan washed and Pete and Kate dried. Pete glanced out through the kitchen window. He whispered into the living room for everyone to look out back and watch the show. Two deer, a raccoon and a skunk were making short work of the leftovers.

The Jenkins cottage was back to normal in fifteen minutes. Everyone thanked Mr. and Mrs. Jenkins and set off down the hill for the beach portion of the party.

———

The last embers of the bonfire crackled sending small puffs of white smoke into the clear, star-filled sky.

"Anyone else want a marshmallow?" Kate asked, holding a sharpened cedar branch in the air.

"Not me," Jane Blair said standing. "I'm full and it's got to be close to midnight. We'd better get back to Kate's."

Ann Early turned from the log she was sitting on to put her guitar back in its case. "Anyone have a last song they want to play before I tuck *Henrietta* into her box?"

The other two guitar players, Duke and Eddie, shook their heads. "I played the only two songs I know," Eddie laughed. "How about you, Duke?"

"No," Duke smiled. "I don't think the girl's hearts can stand any more."

"In your dreams, Duke," Peggy chuckled. "Really, though, you guys were unusually lethargic tonight. Maybe the fish really were bad."

Everyone looked at Neal and stifled a laugh. Neal had eaten all but two filets on the last tray.

"I'm a growing boy. I can't help it," Neal groaned. "Besides, I told you. It was my aunt that said the fish around here weren't any good. She was wrong, that's all. It's not my fault. Now, get off my back."

"Did anyone hear that?" Peggy asked in mock astonishment. "Neal almost condescended."

"Fish really must be brain food," Stella chipped in.

"Neal's IQ has probably shot up thirty points since dinner," Jane smiled.

"All right!" Neal said in a huff. "I'll give you ladies a ride back to Kate's in the *White Cap*. Anything to change the subject."

"No, that's okay," Dan laughed. "Pete and I will take them in my boat. Come on, Kate. We'll run up to the Jenkins' and get our serving dishes. You guys can put out the fire and set up the sleeping bags."

All six came up inside the wood-planked raft.

CHAPTER 21
SKINNY DIP

Wednesday, July 9, 11:45 p.m.

"It's too hot to sleep," Eddie said as the six boys spread their sleeping bags on the beach.

"How about going for a dip?" Pete suggested. "We can swim out to the raft to cool off. I do it all the time on nights like this."

"I can't," John said. "I didn't bring my swim suit."

"So what," Eddie laughed. "It's midnight. Who's going to see us? Come on. Last one in's a twink."

All six boys raced to pull off their socks, shoes, pants, and shirts. The moon was just rising over the top of LaSalle Island as six naked bodies ran out to where the water was deep enough to swim. They raced another thirty yards to the raft that was anchored just past the line of reeds. They splashed and dunked each other until Duke glanced up and caught a glimpse of a small boat approaching from the Elliot dock.

"Hold it. Someone's coming," he said pointing.

All the laughing and splashing stopped. Each of the boys grabbed an edge of the platform and watched the canoe come across the bay.

118

"I bet it's the burglar," Eddie whispered.

That was good enough for Pete. "Hurry," he said as he swam around to the back side of the raft. He was quickly followed by the other five.

"Go on," Neal argued, "it could be anyone."

"Like who?" Duke asked.

"Like anyone. A fisherman," Neal said.

"Yes," Duke said, "or the burglar."

"It could be my dad," Eddie offered. Everyone maneuvered to see over the top of the platform. "He might have decided to come down here to check up on us."

"Could be some of the girls," Duke kidded.

"It better not be," John said seriously. "I'm really not dressed for company. If it's Peggy, she wouldn't speak to me for the rest of the summer."

"Now, wouldn't that be a tragedy?" Neal smirked, remembering Peggy's verbal attack on him at the dinner table.

"Here's what we'll do," Pete whispered. "We'll duck underwater and come up inside the platform. It's pretty grody in there, lots of spiders and cobwebs and stuff; but at least we'll be able to see who it is."

"Spiders?" Neal whispered in alarm. "Not this cowboy! I'm swimming back to shore."

"Come on, Neal," Duke said grabbing him by his mop of blond-white hair. "Just once, join the team. If you don't stay here and we do, the game will be up for the rest of us. Look, you want to see who this guy is, don't you?"

"Not particularly," Neal said. He scowled as the others stared at him. "Oh, all right, but I'm not liking it."

"Let's go," Dan whispered, "he's coming."

All six ducked down and came up inside with about a foot of headroom beneath the wood-plank raft. There was just enough space for all of them to line up along the side facing the approaching boat. Twelve eyes were riveted to the opening between the two sideboard planks. The moon shone clearly on the canoe. The lone paddle dipped mechanically two strokes on the left and two on the right. Whoever it was kept a dead straight course and never made the least bit of splash as he paddled toward them.

"You can bet it's not the girls," John breathed.

"Nor my dad," Eddie added. "He's good with a canoe, but not this good."

"That leaves three likely choices," Duke said, "the French trapper, the Irish lumberjack, and the Indian renegade. I wouldn't want to be caught here by any of them."

"It could be a fisherman," Neal reminded them.

"Well, we're about to find out," Duke whispered. "He's heading directly for us."

The canoe came to within thirty feet of the raft.

"He's turning," Pete said. "He's going toward the Davis boathouse."

"Can anyone tell who it is?" Eddie asked.

"Not from here," Dan said. "He's wearing a hunting cap, though."

"Once he passes those reeds," Eddie said, "I'm for getting back to shore as quick as we can."

"I'm with you," John agreed. "I'm not telling anyone. Let's forget this ever happened."

"We can't do that," Pete said as the canoe disappeared behind the reeds. "We've got to tell my dad. If we don't and Doctor Davis' boathouse gets robbed, people are going to think we did it. The sheriff already suspects kids are behind the break-ins."

"I'll agree to just about anything to get out from under this spider trap," Neal said, pulling cobwebs from his hair. He took a deep breath and slipped underwater.

The other five followed breast-stroking silently into shore. Pete, Dan, and Eddie grabbed some towels and dried off. They pulled on their pants and ran barefoot up to Pete's cabin.

Pete went inside while Dan and Eddie stood outside on the porch in the moonlight.

"We think it's the boathouse burglar, Dad," Pete said, gasping for breath.

"Did you actually see him go into the Davis boathouse?" Howard Jenkins asked.

"Well, not exactly. But he was heading straight for it."

"You're sure he didn't just go past?"

"No," Pete answered. "But where else would he be going?"

"I don't know," Howard Jenkins said. "Could you see who it was?"

"It was a man. He had a man's hat on, anyway—the kind lumbermen or hunters wear."

"Pete, I'm not going to awaken Doctor Davis at one in the morning to tell him someone might be in his boathouse. You know Doc. Except for the *Pal*, he doesn't keep anything in there. Now listen. I'm glad you came to me about this, but I don't see that getting him up at this time of night will accomplish anything. I'll talk to him tomorrow. How come your hair's all wet? You boys weren't skinny dipping, were you?"

"Well, yeah, kind of. It was awful hot."

"Look. I want you to go back down to the beach and stay put. I'll talk to Doctor Davis in the morning."

Pete met Dan and Eddie on the front porch and started down the stairs to the lake. "He says to go to sleep and not do anything foolish," Pete reported.

The short swim had cooled everyone sufficiently; and, with the burglar possibly nearby, they decided to sack out in Pete's boathouse for the night. Pete lit a kerosene lantern while everyone arranged their sleeping bags on the floor.

———

"Hey, Pete," Dan nudged his shoulder. "Are you asleep?"

"No, why?" Pete whispered back.

"Eddie and I are going to row over to the Davis boathouse. Care to join us?"

"I can't. I promised my dad I wouldn't move."

"You don't have to," Dan whispered, shaking his head. "You just have to get into the boat. Eddie'll row. The boat will do all the moving."

Pete rolled his eyes. "I don't think that's what my dad had in mind. Besides, what if we get really lucky and run into this guy?"

"Look," Dan said. "There's three of us to one of him. What can he do?"

"I'm not all that curious to find out," Pete replied, "but I'll bet he'd think of something."

"If we don't go right now," Eddie insisted, "he could get away."

"That would be fine by me," Pete mumbled. "And the farther the better."

"Come on, Pete," Dan argued. "Where's your sense of adventure?"

"I left it on Mackinac," Pete said weakly. And that was for sure.

"Pete," Dan insisted, "we need your help."

"What for?"

"Numbers," Dan said. "There's strength in numbers. Remember what the Cedarville team did to Neal when they put three people on him?"

Pete remembered and nodded. For some reason, explaining unrelated events in basketball terms could convince Pete to do practically anything. Pete got to his feet.

In minutes, the three had slipped out of Pete's shed, walked down the long dock, and stepped into the aluminum boat. Eddie rowed, the oars creaking loudly with every stroke to the front of the Davis boathouse.

Dan, from the bow, pulled the *Tiny Tin* inside and shined his flashlight around the walls. Doc Davis's speedboat, the *Pal*, sat motionless in the still water. Nothing was out of place.

"No sign of anyone here," Dan reported.

"How about that next boathouse?" Eddie asked, nodding over to the ramshakled, green building another twenty yards away.

In a flash, Pete remembered its door being off kilter the morning he caught his trophy bass. "I wonder," he said. "There's nothing in there to steal, but it would be a heck of a place for someone to hide."

"Let's just take a peek. Come on," Dan urged.

"Why me?" Pete mumbled. "All right, but if we're going, Eddie, you'd better let me row. We won't sneak up on anyone with all the racket you make."

"Fine by me," Eddie agreed, and the two traded seats.

Dan pushed the tin boat away from the Davis dock, and Pete pulled the oars silently toward the next boathouse.

"I rowed the tin boat to the Davis boathouse."

CHAPTER 22
PROOF

Thursday, July 10 10:00 a.m.

"All I can tell you, Con," Howard Jenkins said, standing outside the township building, "is what Pete and his friends told me."

"Kids," Sheriff Shoberg shook his head. "They've got more imagination than sense. Right now, I'm busy tracking down leads on the basketball money that was stolen the other night. The man responsible for that is a dangerous person. He could have killed the doctor. I'll have to put the boathouse burglar aside for awhile."

"Who's to say it's not the same person?" Howard asked.

"You've got a point there, Howard. Well, I'll come over and look around, but I'm not expecting much."

"To tell you the truth," Mr. Jenkins said, "I didn't at first either, but I got to wondering, `Why should I doubt them? There've been petty thefts all over the Snows this summer.' So, I rowed over to the old boathouse this morning before coming here. I looked inside.

Trash was everywhere. I didn't want to disturb any-thing, so I came right to you."

"Why didn't you say so in the first place?" Con re-plied. "Where's your boat? We'll go right now."

"Thanks," Howard said, turning toward the dock. "I'd sure hate to think a burglar has been living right under my nose all this time and I didn't have a clue."

The sheriff and Pete's dad boarded the *Flossy* and moved quickly out of Cedarville Bay. They pulled up ten minutes later at the Jenkins' dock. Pete was wait-ing to help them tie up.

"So, Pete," Sheriff Shoberg began, "when did all this happen?"

"About midnight, I guess. We were having a sleepover on our beach, but it was so hot, we had to go for a swim. The six of us swam out to the raft, and we saw this guy go past in a canoe toward the Davis dock. We swam back to shore and I told my dad. A few min-utes later Dan, Eddie, and I rowed the tin boat to the Davis boathouse to see if the guy was there; but he wasn't. So then Dan said, 'How about the next boat-house?'"

"Who's this `Dan' you're talking about?" Sheriff Shoberg asked, taking a pad and pencil from his jacket pocket.

"Dan Hinken," Pete said. "He lives along Cincin-nati Row. He's incredible. Every time he gets a hunch, he's right. So, anyway, we head over to Long's boat-house. The door there's on a tilt—ice damage, I guess—and Dan sticks his head inside. He shines his flashlight around. I hear him whistle and he says, `Let's get out of here.' I turn around and row for all I'm worth. We get back here to the dock and he tells us that there's

125

all sorts of stuff in there—beer cans, food wrappers, stuff like that. That's it, Sheriff. That's all I know."

"All right," Con Shoberg said. "Let's take a look. We'll use your aluminum boat since we know it'll fit under the boathouse entrance."

The three set out with Mr. Shoberg in the bow, Howard Jenkins rowing, and Pete in the stern. Once inside, the police officer lifted himself onto the deck. In two minutes, he'd collected pieces of evidence and reboarded the *Tiny Tin*.

"Nothing's real fresh," he said thoughtfully. "It's been a few days by the looks of things, but there's no doubt someone was staying here. Say, this door is on an odd tilt," he said as he inspected the entrance more closely. "And look, there are some fresh scratch marks on the hinge. It's like someone wrenched it up so he could get in. The person who did that has to be mighty strong. Pete, I don't want you or your friends to do any more detective work. You were lucky last night that you didn't catch the guy red-handed. It's my guess that whoever is doing this is desperate. I've got three suspects. I'll tell you this, Pete, if you push any one of them into a corner, you'll be in for an adventure you wouldn't even wish on your mean, big sister," he said with a smile. "If you see anything at all, I want you to come straight to me. You read?"

"Yes, sir," Pete nodded, and he had every intention of doing exactly that.

*She weaved back and
forth over the boat's wake.*

CHAPTER 23
SKI LESSON

Thursday, July 10 1:30 p.m.

"Would you like to go skiing, Pete?" Kate asked as she stood on the Jenkins' porch with Dan and Eddie. "It's too hot for sunbathing, and there's not enough wind to sail."

"Sure, but I've never skied before," Pete said, standing at the door holding a bowl of alphabet soup. "Is it hard to learn?"

"You've never skied?" Eddie asked.

"Nope, but I'd like to learn," Pete replied.

"My dad's letting us use the *Silver Moon*," Eddie said. "She's great to ski behind. It'll pop you right out of the water."

"I'm game. It can't be any worse than sailing," Pete laughed, remembering his first, skull-cracking lesson on the *Griffin*. "I've got to finish lunch and do a couple quick chores. How about if I meet you at your place in half an hour?"

"Bring a swimming suit and towel," Kate said turning toward the porch steps. "We'll see you then."

"Where're we headed?" Pete asked as Eddie hit the starter button on the Terkel's new, mahogany speedboat.

The engine roared reverberating through the red, double boathouse rafters. Eddie checked the throttle down to shifting range and slid her into reverse. "Over to Muscallonge Bay off Arnold Point. It should be dead calm over there, and it's out of the way from other boat traffic. There are usually no fishermen or anyone else to get in the way."

Five minutes later, the Chris-Craft runabout had thundered across Elliot Bay, passed Connors Point, and slowed in front of a mansion of a boathouse on the northern point of Little LaSalle Island.

"We'll take turns," Eddie said as he idled the engine in neutral. "Kate, you can go first."

Dan tossed the two wooden skis into the water beside the boat as Eddie fastened the tow rope to the chrome ring on the *Silver Moon*'s stern. Pete couldn't help staring as Kate removed her terry cloth robe and strapped the ski belt around her waist. She was tall and slender and had a terrific build. She smiled as Pete stood there, his mouth agape like a kid watching a magic show. She stepped up on the starboard gunwale, paused for a moment, and then dived head first, barely making a splash.

She bobbed to the surface, shook her long, blond hair, and smiled at the three boys.

"How's the water, Kate?" Dan asked.

"Brisk," she replied and went to work slipping her feet into the rubber ski shoes.

"We'll start with a couple small circles," Eddie called out as he eased the *Silver Moon* ahead. "Chapman's boathouse will be the drop-off point, okay?"

Kate waved back and let the tow line slide through her hands. With everything in place, she took hold of the handle. The line went taut and she poked the ski tips out of the water.

"Ready," she yelled.

Eddie gunned the throttle. The *Silver Moon*'s 158-horsepower engine churned the water and the sleek craft surged ahead.

Kate popped up on the wooden slats and headed outside the wake even before it had formed, a trick she could do that neither Eddie nor Dan could manage.

Pete sat in awe as she weaved back and forth flying over the boat's wake, her skis slapping on the froth. They soon approached the end of the first circle in front of the immense, brown boathouse. Eddie watched for trouble ahead as he steered the course, while Dan kept his eyes on Kate relaying her hand signals to Eddie.

Kate raised her index finger. Dan called to Eddie, "She's dropping a ski, Eddie. Pete, watch to see where it goes. We'll have to retrieve it when she's done."

Kate wiggled her left foot out of the rubber boot, and the discarded ski hydroplaned across the front of the five-stall boathouse. It coasted to a halt about thirty feet in front of the last entrance. Pete marked the spot by noting that it was floating near the lopsided door of the smallest boat well. He quickly turned his attention back to Kate. She was slaloming now with even more daring and acrobatic grace than she had on two skis. Eventually, she waved her forefinger in a large circle and then drew a line across her throat.

"One more loop, Eddie," Dan yelled, "and then she wants in."

"Okay," Eddie called out over the roar of the engine.

He made another circuit and then guided the *Silver Moon* toward the boathouse at full speed. Kate went to the inside of the circle and then slashed across behind the boat and flew over the outside wake letting go of the rope as she landed. She skimmed past four of the boathouse entrances and then sank into the water not more than a foot from the ski she had dropped on the first pass. Eddie spun the steering wheel. The engine roared as the propeller turned out of the water. The *Silver Moon* quickly came alongside Kate.

"That was really something, Kate," Pete said.

"Thanks," Kate grinned. Her cheeks and lips had turned an odd, bluish tint. "It's great fun. You'll see. Now, it's your turn. I'll stay in the water to help you get started. Hop in."

Dan handed a ski belt to Pete and tied it around his waist. Pete stepped up on the side of the boat and looked over the edge. It suddenly occurred to him that, for all the years he'd been coming to the Snows, he'd never gone swimming anywhere other than the shallow water of Elliot Bay. Although the water was always brutally cold in June, by July it was, if not warm, at least tolerable. He paused as he peered into the deep, blue vortex in front of him. The shade and depth should have been a warning. It certainly wasn't a Honolulu Blue. It was more of an Arctic Silver-Blue. The water appeared to crystalize right before his eyes. *What the heck*, he thought, *if Kate can take it, it can't be that cold.*

He teetered on the side and then jumped, feet first into Muscallonge Bay. From the moment his toes touched the surface, he knew he'd made a mistake. *Brisk?* Pete thought at once. *What kind of cruel trick is this? This can't be water. It has to be anti-freeze. Water can't get this cold.*

He was still going down when he realized why drowned sailors were never recovered in the northern Great Lakes. They'd freeze instantly and sink like anchors. He was still plunging downward when he realized that he would never come up. Ever. The pressure inside his head crashed on the bridge of his nose. His lungs were about to burst when he noticed the light growing brighter. His head broke the surface; he gasped for air.

"Holy Hannah," he screamed.

Eddie and Dan broke into hysterics. Kate could barely keep her head above water.

"You've got to be joking!" Pete exclaimed. "You can't expect me to stay in here. Get serious!"

"Oh, come on, Pete. It's not that bad," Kate said swimming alongside. She snuggled up close and put her arms around his chest.

Pete jerked his shoulders up straight and blinked his eyes. *Well, now,* Pete thought. *Kate might be right. This isn't so bad, after all. The water seems to be getting warmer already.*

She grabbed the tow rope as it passed by. "Okay, Pete, this is important," she said softly in his ear. "You saw what I did. Just keep the handle close to your chest and your knees bent. When Eddie hits the gas, stay crouched until you get some speed and then push your feet down. You'll stand right up. Once you're going, keep your knees flexed, your arms straight, and lean back. The boat will do the rest. Okay?"

"Yeah. Sure. Okay." Pete's teeth were chattering.

"All right," Kate said. "Here's the end of the rope. Make sure you keep the ski tips out of the water."

"Got it," Pete mumbled. *Okay. Stay crouched. Knees bent. Tips up. Okay. Okay.* "Go, Eddie!"

Pete smiled confidently to Kate and then set his sights ahead. Just as the line snapped out of the water he noticed that the tip of his right ski had slipped below the surface. The *Silver Moon* bolted ahead and Pete's left ski popped on top of the water. His right ski, however, dived straight into the depths of Muscallonge Bay. Every muscle, sinew, and bone in Pete's body stretched to a snapping point as he held on for dear life. He slashed across the surface, torrents of water crashing into his face. Finally, he could hold on no longer. The rope handle ripped from his fingers. The line flew like a sling shot toward the rapidly disappearing *Silver Moon*. Pete plummeted downward, once again, into the freezing depths. Water shot into his nose and mouth. It burst through his ears in an explosion of pain.

Had it not been for the ski belt, Pete would have joined Fats at the bottom of Lake Huron. He finally bobbed to the surface. As he lifted his head to gulp a breath of air, he opened his eyes just as a wall of water put up by the returning *Silver Moon* smashed into his face. It gushed into his lungs. Pete coughed uncontrollably, gasping and choking before he could catch his breath.

"Pete, are you all right?" Kate shouted between strokes as she swam to his side.

"Oh, yeah, I'm just fine," Pete said between gasping for air and throwing up mouthfuls of letter-shaped spaghetti bits. "Yeah, that was great fun. What's next? Barrel riding over the Tahquamenon Falls? Hey, look. I'm done. Just let me get back in the boat."

"Oh, come on, Pete," Kate laughed. "You can't quit now. Everyone does that on the first try. This time you'll do great. You'll see."

"You might have told me."

"If I had, you wouldn't have done it."

"I certainly can't argue with that. Maybe we should just take a few days to let my arms and legs realign themselves with their sockets."

"You're not going to get off that easy," Kate said, watching the *Silver Moon* approach. "Eddie's coming. I've got your other ski. Here. Slip it on. Really, Pete, you almost had it."

"You're right. I almost <u>did</u> have it. And now, whatever it was I almost had, I know I don't want. Look, just help me get back in the boat and you three can ski all afternoon. I won't get in anyone's way or ask for cuts or anything, I promise."

"Nope," Kate stiffened. "If you don't try once more, I'll never speak to you again."

An idle threat, Pete thought, *but I can't take the chance.* "Okay, but if I die, I'll never forgive you."

Kate grabbed the handle and held it as the *Silver Moon* drifted by in neutral. She waited as Pete got his feet in the ski boots and then gave him the handle. Pete went through the checklist. *Ski tips up, knees bent, arms close to the chest,* "Okay, Eddie!" he yelled with noticeably less enthusiasm that on his first attempt.

The *Silver Moon* churned forward. This time Pete was too scared to make a mistake. He popped up, both skis heading pretty much in the same direction. After the first few terrifying moments, he looked around and realized what a thrill it was to be standing on the water traveling at close to the speed of light. It was like sledding down an icy hill back home at Hoyt Park. He was in control only as long as nothing really bad happened. He held on grinning hysterically as he followed the speedboat in its large circle around Muscallonge Bay.

On the second pass he thought he might try to slide over to the other side of the speedboat's wake. This was a brave move, indeed. He got to the huge wave and immediately caught the inside edge of his right ski on the crest. He teetered momentarily, regained his balance, and eased himself back to the froth directly behind the boat. That was as adventurous as he was going to get. He'd be glad to finish the circle and slide into the drop-off point in front of the boathouse.

Having decided this, he looked thirty feet ahead and realized that he was skiing straight into the path of two, four-foot high swells that had been put up by the *Silver Moon* on his first circuit. Each crest was approaching from different angles. The confrontation was unavoidable.

One second, Pete was right-side up cruising along on two skis. The next, he was upside down, skis, arms, and legs slashing at the air in six directions. He flew high out of the water. In a primal scream of terror, he plunged toward the lake. He hit the surface head first at an unbelievable rate of speed. His mouth filled with water. His cheeks wrapped around to the back of his head. He bounded once, twice. On the third slap, he flew again, high into the air. He opened his eyes and watched as he approached the horizon. He plunged through it like a spear at a lake trout.

Dan yelled and Eddie spun the steering wheel. The *Silver Moon* turned dangerously on its side cutting back toward Pete. Kate was nowhere around as she watched from the other side of the bay in front of the Chapman boathouse. If Pete survived this fall, there'd be no talking him into another try. The *Silver Moon* came alongside. Dan reached down and pulled Pete into the boat. Pete found Kate's terry cloth robe and immediately wrapped himself inside. He shivered on the floor at Eddie's feet making himself into as small a ball as would seem humanly possible.

Eddie swung the speedboat over to the crash site, and Dan picked up the skis, which had ended up about fifty yards apart. Eddie then raced over in front of the boathouse where Kate was still treading water.

"Way to go, Pete," she yelled. "Wasn't that great?"

Great hadn't entered his mind. **Horrendous**, yes. **Life-threatening**, of course. But **great**? Never. Not in a million years.

Kate pulled herself aboard. She glanced around for her robe but recognized that Pete might not give it up without a fight. Dan tossed her a towel and she dried off.

Pete looked up as Dan dived, head first, into Muscallonge Bay. His head popped out of the water. He smiled back to his friends like he'd just jumped into a Caribbean lagoon.

How do they do that? Pete wondered.

Dan slid his skis on and buckled the life belt Kate handed him. She motioned for Eddie to ease ahead.

"Let her rip, Eddie!" Dan called out. And they were off. Pete watched as Dan went a few times around Muscallonge Bay. Finally, Dan let go of the rope and slid to a stop in front of the Chapman boathouse.

Then it was Eddie's turn. Kate took the driver's seat and Dan watched for Eddie's signals. Eddie flashed in and out of the wake, skiing forwards and backwards and slaloming at ever increasing speeds.

Each time around, though, even in his misery, Pete couldn't help but noticing how extraordinary the brown boathouse was. It was not only immense, it was majestic. It had all sorts of alcoves and nooks and niches with five openings for boats; the one in the center could have held an ocean liner. It was like a castle on water. All of its entrances, however, were closed and its windows shuttered.

"Who'd you say owns that boathouse?" Pete asked Dan.

"The Chapman Family," Dan yelled over the roar of the *Silver Moon*'s engine. "They're from Chicago. They've got a really nice place overlooking Lake Huron on Little LaSalle, but they keep their boats here."

"How come it's all boarded up," Pete hollered back.

"They're in Europe this summer," Dan replied. "They didn't even bring their boats out of storage."

Eddie climbed out of the water and towelled himself dry. "Let's head home," he said. "It's almost time for dinner."

Pete had warmed up just enough to keep his jaws from rattling. His lips, though, were still cyanotic and felt as if they belonged on someone else's face—a much older person's face. As Eddie took control of the *Silver Moon*, he looked for traffic and shifted the gear forward. Pete noticed again that the smallest door on the Chapman boathouse was slightly askew. He recognized, however, that this couldn't be ice damage and neglect like the Long boathouse in Elliot Bay. This boathouse was in perfect condition except for the tilted door. Something else must have caused it. As for what,

Pete hadn't a clue. Maybe it had something to do with what Sheriff Shoberg had told him that morning.

He was about to ask Dan what he thought about it when Eddie hit the throttle. The roar of the engine cut off any possible conversation. Pete, as numb as he was, decided it couldn't be all that important, anyway.

In five minutes the *Silver Moon* was making its approach to the red, double boathouse in Cedarville Channel.

"Pete, are you all right?"

CHAPTER 24
THE AUDIENCE

Thursday, July 10   2:20 p.m.

What's making all the racket? Fats thought, snapping awake from a deep sleep. *Someone's coming.* Even within the shuttered barn of a boathouse, Fats could tell it was full daylight. During the past week he'd made himself fairly comfortable in the upstairs loft of the mammoth building. He rolled in his bunk, the creaking of the cot springs echoed off the walls. The rhythmic, rolling wake of a powerful boat plowed through the stone crib docks of its five entrances.

The deafening thunder of the *Silver Moon* made Fats jump right out of his bed. The throttle cut back and the engine came to an idle seemingly right below him. He glanced to his right to see if Mickey was awake. His cot was empty; he was gone. Fats looked down over the railing beside him into the boat well. Mickey often went on midnight raids, scavenging boathouses for food, but he was always back by sunrise. Fats' eyes adjusted to the light. The canoe was missing. *That lousy, Irish double-crosser. He's gone into town and turned me into the cops. The sheriff is out-side right now.*

Fats' eyes darted through the boathouse in panic. He scrambled down the ladder and rushed to a door that lead to the outside dock and to the island forest beyond. He shook the handle, but it was, as he knew it would be, dead-bolted and double-key locked. This boathouse was built as solid as Fort Mackinac. He raced back up to the loft. Through the only unshuttered window in the whole building, Fats scanned the area in front of him. This time he looked more carefully into the bay for the sheriff.

A large, mahogany speedboat sat in the water not thirty yards in front of him. Two boys were standing in the stern looking intently over the side at a boy and a girl who seemed to have been thrown overboard. No, they were struggling with two boards and a rope.

As Fats' eyes gradually adjusted to the light, he realized that it wasn't the sheriff after all. Only water skiers. Kids.

He looked again. These weren't just any kids. They were the same ones he had chased from Mackinac Island the week before! Luck finally had come his way. His brief elation quickly turned to resentment. Why should they be so carefree while he was so miserable? He was living like an animal, sleeping in bat-infested boathouses while they frolicked in the summer sun.

Fats' mind was racing. *I'm going to bring a little misery into their lives. That speedboat's got a name on it. If they just pull around, I'll be able to read it. It has to belong somewhere nearby, and I'll track 'em down. There, the girl is helping that scruffy kid get up on the skis. He's the one I had in my sights before I was blown out of the boat. Hah! He took a nose-dive. I hope he drowns. There he goes again; they're coming around. It's the Silver Moon. Now, to wait until they're done.*

Finally, they're quitting. The big, dark-haired kid is behind the wheel and heading out past the lighted buoy. They're going around the other point and down the channel. I'll get my chance one of these nights to find out where they live; and when I do, I'll put an end to them. After that I'll finish off Mickey and the Frenchman. Then no one will be able to track me. I'll slip across the border into Canada and start a whole new life.

Pete pulled up to his dock in Elliot Bay.

CHAPTER 25
NEAL'S CHANCE

Thursday, July 10   4:30 p.m.

Eddie guided the *Silver Moon* into the left-hand side of the red, double boathouse just as the *White Cap* roared toward them from town. Neal Preston slammed the engine into reverse and coasted up to the returning skiers. Dan and Kate hopped out of the *Silver Moon* putting dock lines to the pilings.

"What's up, Neal?" Eddie asked.

"Our boathouse was broken into again last night," Neal hollered. "The guy stole my sleeping bag. I was planning on getting you and Dan to camp out with me over in Duck Bay this week, Eddie. I'm going to get that miserable slug if it's the last thing I do. You don't have anything new on him, do you?"

"No," Eddie replied. "The last thing we heard is what Mrs. Schoolcraft told us at the township hall. But you know all about that."

"Well," Kate said, putting a bow line to the dock, "I'm going to run up and change for dinner."

"Me, too," Eddie said. "Toss me that stern line, Pete. Have you warmed up yet?"

"Yeah, some," Pete said as he unwrapped himself from Kate's robe and handed it to her.

"We'll see you later, Neal," Kate said.

Dan followed Kate and Eddie out of the boathouse. "Great job for your first time skiing, Pete," Dan said. "We'll give it another go soon. Maybe tomorrow."

"Yeah. Maybe," Pete said, trying to sound appreciative. "Thanks for the lesson."

When the three had left and Pete and Neal were alone, Pete pulled his tee-shirt over his head. He looked over at Neal. "You were asking about the burglar?"

Neal just stared at Pete. "*What a moron*," he seemed to say with a sneer and a nod of his head.

"Well," Pete continued, "I saw something this afternoon that was a little strange. I'm not really sure if it means anything, but that huge boathouse over there on Little LaSalle, some Chicago family owns it . . ."

"You obviously mean The Chapmans, The *William T.* Chapmans, the wealthiest family in Chicago."

"Yeah, that's it, the Chapmans. They couldn't make it up here this summer. Anyway, one of their boathouse doors was off-kilter. The odd thing is is that it sort of reminded me of the old boathouse down in Elliot Bay. The sheriff said the burglar might have wrenched that boathouse door up and used the place as a hideout for a couple of weeks. The guy's gone now, though," Pete shrugged. "It's probably nothing."

"No," Neal muttered. "Coming from you, it IS nothing." Neal turned to start the *White Cap*'s engine. Suddenly, he whirled around and stared at Pete like he'd

142

been smacked from behind by a polo mallet. "Look," Neal said quickly, "it's been fun, our little chat and all, but I've got to go." He shoved his boat away from the dock and pushed the starter. The *White Cap* roared and Neal spun the wheel aiming his speedboat back towards town.

Pete watched for a moment, shook his head, and then went out of the boathouse and hopped in the *Tiny Tin*. He untied the two lines and pulled the starter cord. It coughed twice and on the third try, it fired. He headed home exhausted from his brief but adventurous ski lesson. He was still numb, either from the frigid water or the trauma of his two dramatic spills. He never wanted to see a pair of skis again. Life would be so much easier if Kate didn't enjoy so many terrifying activities. If he was going to remain a part of her circle of friends, however, he'd have to keep up with her. Besides, he had a strong suspicion that she might not think shooting BB's at tin cans at the island dump would be much sport. It was fun, though. And it could be dangerous, too. Kate seemed to thrive on life-and-death situations. Not only was there broken glass everywhere, but if a mother bear and a couple of her cubs wandered along . . . . Or a skunk. He'd never forget that day. Pete still couldn't look a glass of tomato juice in the eye—and that was five years ago.

As Pete passed the last boathouse in Cincinnati Row, he was daydreaming so hard about Kate that he nearly drove the *Tiny Tin* smack into the Elliot Hotel dock—full speed—broad daylight.

He jerked the steering handle to the left in the last split-second and swerved around it. He'd never, ever, done that before. *I've got to be more careful*, he thought. *This would be a terrible time to die. I've got too much to live for.*

As Pete pulled up to his dock in Elliot Bay, he looked across and saw the *White Cap* racing back from Cedarville toward Urie Point. Neal's blond hair glistened in the sun as he sat alone at the wheel.

Pete turned toward shore and headed up the steps to his cottage for dinner.

The sun had set on the Les Cheneaux Islands.

CHAPTER 26
THE PLOT

Thursday, July 10   10:00 p.m.

The sun had set and darkness was nearly complete in the Les Cheneaux Islands. Fats remained at the loft window were he had watched the kids skiing almost five hours before. He still hadn't seen Mickey from the previous night. If the Irishman hadn't gone to the cops, then where was he? He wouldn't have left all his belongings if he wasn't coming back.

In the distance, along the reed-lined shore of Urie Bay, Fats spotted the silhouette of a canoe making its way toward him in the moonlight. He hurried down the ladder to the last boat well. Five minutes later, it's bow slid under the tilted boathouse door.

Fats heard a click, and the beam of a small flashlight ricocheted around the parlor area. He could see it was Mickey and that he was alone.

"Hey, Fats," Mickey growled from the stern of the canoe. "Where are you?"

"I'm here," Fats said, stepping out from the shadows. "Where have YOU been?"

145

"Putting grub on the table," Mickey barked. "I left before sun-up, got into a boathouse in Bosely Channel, and by the time I'd gotten everything out, it was just turning light. I looked around and, between there and here, three fishing boats had set their anchors. I couldn't get past them without being seen, so I decided not to try. I slipped my canoe back through the reeds and came ashore. I sacked out in the woods all day. Lucky thing I found a good sleeping bag in the Bosely Channel boathouse. Got this little flashlight, too. Hey, I bet you thought I'd run out on you. Right?"

"It occurred to me," Fats grumbled. "Say, do you know where a speedboat called the *Silver Moon* is kept?

"Yeah. Red, double boathouse on Big LaSalle. I got some stuff out of there a week ago. In fact, it was the same night I found you. What of it?"

"Nothing," Fats said. "I just saw it go by today, that's all."

"Well, let's see what's on today's menu, eh," Mickey said, moving toward the canvas bag in the middle of the canoe. "Give me a hand, will you?"

As Fats reached for the cloth sack he heard something bump the boathouse door. He ducked down and looked under the entrance. Another scratch and the bow of a small boat popped inside. It was the prow of a dinghy.

"Hey, someone's trying to get in," Fats whispered. "You were followed. Douse the light, Mickey. Fast."

"I'll get him," Mickey said as he scrambled out of the canoe. The inside of the boathouse was pitch black. Mickey stepped over to where the dinghy was forcing itself inside.

146

Pierre LeSoeur's camp on Bass Cove Lake.

CHAPTER 27
THE SET-UP

Thursday, July 10 10:15 p.m.

With Mickey staying behind to finish off the blond-haired kid, Fats slid the canoe out of the Chapman boathouse and paddled toward Bosely Channel. The bright canopy of stars provided plenty of light to guide him into the open water of Lake Huron. He turned east as Mickey had instructed and saw the marsh where he had been blown from his speedboat not two weeks before. He kept his canoe close to Big LaSalle Island dodging jagged, room-sized boulders that pierced the surface from the black depths.

He drew his paddle smoothly through the rolling, Lake Huron swells and watched carefully for the odd landmark Mickey had described. According to the Irishman, the shoreline treetops would suddenly disappear deep into the woods. That was the sign that he had reached Bass Cove Lake, the site of Pierre LeSoeur's camp.

Fats paddled over a mile from Bosely channel before he caught sight of the landmark. He then rowed ashore and dragged the canoe onto the pebbly beach. He stepped through the long reeds crouching as he went. In the distance he saw the dying embers of a campfire on the far side of the island lake. He checked the direction of the light breeze. He would attack upwind.

Fats knelt on one knee allowing his eyes to adjust to the flickering light. Across the lake he saw the stocky Frenchman stretched out on the ground with his arms crossed and his feet practically touching the glowing coals. Pierre's head was slumped forward, his back leaning against a fallen pine.

Fats took ten minutes to work his way around the shoreline. He approached Pierre's campsite. The trapper took a swig from a pottery jar he held between his knees. Across his lap, the Frenchman cradled *Antoinette*, his primitive, double-barreled shotgun.

Then, slowly, Pierre's head drifted backwards. His lower jaw dropped open; his head bobbed twice against the fallen cedar.

Fats stepped forward through the few remaining reeds into a clearing. He was fifteen feet away from Pierre and could feel the warmth of the Frenchman's campfire. He watched Pierre's hands slip from the stock of his gun.

Suddenly, just offshore, a resounding splash set Fats' neck hairs on end. A largemouth bass flew out of the water taking a dragonfly in its gaping mouth. It slapped back onto the surface, the echo ringing from shore to shore. Pierre LeSoeur bolted up. He stared into the darkness of the lake clenching his gun.

Fats cowered, stock-still, not fifteen feet behind Pierre in the clearing between Pierre and his cabin. He'd be shot immediately if Pierre looked his way.

Instead, Pierre watched the widening concentric circles where the bass had risen. He sat down and placed *Antoinette* across his lap. He picked up his jar and drank, once again, from its contents. Soon, his head slumped back against the cedar log.

Fats waited for several moments, his heart slamming in his throat, before resuming his approach. He inched forward, step by step. The warmth of the fading coals flushed Fats' forehead. In seconds, he stood, motionless, staring down into Pierre's expressionless face. The Frenchman's head rested peacefully against the cedar trunk, his eyes closed.

Fats drew a heavy, whip-like club from his jacket pocket. He raised it over his head and reached with his left hand for Pierre's shotgun.

Splash! Splash!

Two huge bass came out of the water simultaneously not five feet from shore. Fats and Pierre both jerked from their places. Pierre yanked the trigger and a blast of buckshot flew past Fats' right ear.

Fats dived onto Pierre, grabbing the gun as he did. He tore the stock from the dazed trapper and bounced to his feet. He pointed the barrel into the Frenchman's face and stepped back in the flickering campfire light.

"It's your turn, Frenchy," Fats howled. "Get up. This time, I'm taking you for a ride. You make one twitch, and it'll be your last."

"A dinghy. It could be Neal's.
Yes, it's the Magpie."

CHAPTER 28
DISCOVERY

Thursday, July 10 10:15 p.m.

Pete and his dad had gone out for some late-evening bass fishing; but when the sun went down, the mosquitoes began to get more bites than the fishermen. With three keepers on the stringer, the anglers headed for shore.

The stars shown down on the bay as Pete tied the *Tiny Tin*'s bow line to the dock. Looking up, he noticed a small boat approaching slowly into Elliot Bay. From the bow, a flashlight searched the shoreline.

Pete strained to see into the darkness. "Someone's coming, Dad. I can't tell for sure, but it might be Dan."

"Don't be late, Pete. Tomorrow's kindling day," Howard said as he picked up the stringer of bass and headed toward the cottage.

"Okay. I won't be long."

Dan's red and white Lyman chugged cautiously toward Pete's dock as Eddie, standing in the bow, called back to Dan to go this way and then that.

"Do you see anything?" Dan said softly. His voice carried across the water as though he were already next to the dock.

"Not yet," Eddie answered. "Not with all these reeds."

"It's got to be right here," Kate said. "There. Look," she pointed. "Someone's standing on the end of that pier."

The light flashed along the dock and into Pete's eyes.

"Is that you, Pete?" Dan spoke softly.

"Dan?"

"Yes," Dan replied.

"Who's with you?"

"Eddie and Kate."

"What's up?" Pete asked.

"Neal's missing," Eddie said as Dan cut the engine. "We got a call an hour ago from his parents. Have you seen him?"

"Not since we got back from skiing," Pete said. Dan's boat coasted alongside the dock. Pete continued, "After he told us about his boathouse being broken into, you three went up for dinner. I talked to him for a minute. I told him about the boathouse door we'd seen while we were skiing."

Eddie clicked off the flashlight and the four stood looking at each other. Their eyes adjusted and soon the starlight was all they needed.

"Please?" Dan asked. "What door?"

"The boathouse door," Pete said. "You know, at the Chapman's boathouse over on Little LaSalle."

"No," Dan persisted. "What about it?"

"It was tilted. Like the one over there," Pete said pointing to the Long boathouse. "You remember. Last night after the potluck? We went over to the green

151

boathouse. It had a tilted door. You guys saw it. We talked about it when Sheriff Shoberg was . . ." Pete's jaw dropped. "No, WE didn't talk about it. Sheriff Shoberg and I talked about it. I never told you what he said . . . Holy cow," Pete whispered.

Pete looked nervously into Dan's eyes.

"That's where Neal is now," Dan breathed. "He's at Chapman's boathouse. And he's in trouble."

"Whoa," Eddie said, putting his hands up. "You've lost me. Why's Neal at Chapman's boathouse? And why is he in trouble?"

Dan talked quickly before turning to start the motor. "Pete gave Neal a very important clue to the burglar's new hideout. One that Pete didn't even know himself. Neal put two and two together and, well, you heard him this afternoon. He'll try to get the guy all by himself—just like he tried to play the basketball game—as a one-man team. We've got to find him. Hop in, Pete. We'll need you."

Pete jumped in the red and white Lyman and sat down next to Kate as Dan pulled the starting cord. The Evinrude whined as Dan jammed both the gear and throttle ahead at the same instant.

"We're going to call Sheriff Shoberg, right?" Pete yelled over the roar of the motor.

"There's no time," Dan called back. "It could be an hour before he shows up. I've got a hunch Neal doesn't have an hour."

In minutes, the red and white Lyman was coasting up to the Chapman boathouse with Eddie in the bow, Pete and Kate in the middle, and Dan driving from the stern. Pete pointed to the lopsided door, and Dan nosed the bow up to it as he cut the engine.

"Pete, sit back here," Dan whispered. "Eddie and I are going in. Just pull the bow up to the door, Eddie. Kate, sit back here with Pete."

Pete and Kate moved back from the middle seat as Eddie drew the boat ahead. The bow was a good six inches above the bottom of the door; but Eddie lifted up on the overhang, and the nose slipped under. With the Lyman half inside and half outside, Eddie ducked below the gunwales and squeezed into the monstrous building.

"Hand me your flashlight, Dan," Eddie said, reaching under the door.

A click accompanied a shaft of light which Pete, Dan, and Kate, from outside the boathouse, could only guess what it revealed within.

"What do you see, Eddie?" Dan asked.

"A dinghy. It could be Neal's. Yes, it's the *Magpie*. Neal's here somewhere. Hey, Neal!" Eddie yelled.

The echo bounced throughout the huge building, but there was no response.

"Do you see a canoe?" Dan asked.

"No," Eddie replied. "Just Neal's dinghy. Must be the burglar's gone. Maybe he's taken Neal with him."

"Maybe, but let's search the boathouse, anyway. Kate? I want you and Pete to stay here," Dan said as he slipped to the bottom of the Lyman. He disappeared under the boathouse door and stood up next to Eddie inside the boathouse. Eddie flashed his light throughout the recesses of the cavernous building. Dan climbed a boarding ladder and stood on the boathouse floor.

"I remember a loft at the other end," Dan whispered to Kate and Pete from under the door. "Eddie and I are going to check it out."

Pete could feel the bow rise when Eddie followed Dan out of the boat. The middle of the Lyman stuck firmly on its gunwales to the overhanging door.

Kate glanced around anxiously. "I'm not waiting, Pete," she said. She moved toward the bow. "You stay here. If we're not back in five minutes, take off and get help."

Pete nodded. Kate squeezed under the door and vanished inside.

The last thing Pete wanted to do was to go into that boathouse. The next to the last thing was to be here alone. He wished he'd never mentioned the slanted door to anyone.

A minute passed. The beam of Dan's flashlight faded as the search party explored further into the boathouse. Still, Pete could see its reflection occasionally on the water.

Pete didn't have a watch. It was so dark that he couldn't have read it if he had, but two minutes must have passed. No sound now. No light. He heard a scuffling off in the distance. It was coming from high in the boathouse rafters. He sat quietly, the boat wedged under the door. The only direction it could possibly go would be forward. Pete had no interest in going forward. He only wanted to go back. Way back. Two weeks back.

Five minutes passed.

Pete had never sat still for five minutes in his life. He could troll for hours and not catch anything; he often did. At least he was moving. But he couldn't tolerate still-fishing. Sitting in one place staring at a bobber would drive him crazy. This was worse. In the distance, beyond Urie bay, Pete heard a blast. It could have been kids letting off some fireworks, but it sounded more like a shotgun.

Thick, black cumulus clouds rolled in from the southeast covering the rising moon. The few stars that remained overhead were scarcely enough for Pete to see the boathouse which was no more than two feet in front of his face. He leaned forward and inched toward the bow. He ducked his head down between the middle seat and the door. He peered up into the boathouse. If the outside seemed dark, it was full daylight compared to the inside. He was sure he'd see rays of Dan's flashlight somewhere inside. He lay there, holding his breath—listening—watching.

He groped with his hands for the side of the dock. His eyes gradually adjusted; he caught a faint distinction of gray amidst the world of black. A muffled thump from far away, high in the rafters made him recoil onto the floor of the outboard. Something was dreadfully wrong, but he was too terrified to call out to his friends.

Pete pulled the tiny penlight from his fishing jacket. He knew the battery was nearly dead, but it might flicker long enough to give him a glimmer of light. On the other hand, it might let the burglar know he was there. Maybe that's why he couldn't see Dan's flashlight. The burglar had done something to Dan, Eddie, and Kate. He'd have to go in and find them.

Pete slid further toward the bow. He lifted himself up to the boathouse deck. He crouched for a moment, motionless, hoping to see some sign of his friends.

His heart was racing. He stood up. He felt for the wall and inched forward. In his right hand was the penlight. Should he turn it on? With his left hand, he reached into his other pocket and withdrew his dad's old, hunting knife. He held the handle feeling for the lever with his thumb.

He pressed the penlight. It glimmered faintly.

In the gray-black haze in front of him, Pete thought he could see the outline of a man squatting motionlessly before him facing him square in the face. He was imagining this, he knew, but the shape seemed to be holding a paddle in one hand and, in the other, a huge lantern. Pete heard a click and he practically jumped out of his skin. He was instantly blinded by a brilliant beam of intense light.

Pete spun to his right hearing a low, diabolical laugh. He fell against the wall. The blazing light scorched his eyes.

"Aye, me laddie, I was beginning to think you'd never come out of that boat," Mickey O'Flynn bellowed. "Your mates are up in my playroom. They've been such good little boys and girls, so quiet and still—just like you're going to be, heh, heh."

The Irishman set the lamp on the floor, its mirrored lens penetrating into the center of Pete's consciousness. Mickey stepped forward gripping the paddle. His eyes burrowed into Pete's like Ty Cobb staring down an enemy pitcher. Pete recoiled slowly inching away from the direct beam of the lantern.

He saw the Irishman step toward him. Pete realized that this might be his only chance. He'd rather take it now than not at all. He squeezed the switch on his knife handle and felt the blade snap into position behind his back. He rose to his feet and whipped the knife in front of him. Pete jumped back into the darkness and out of the direct beam of the lantern. As he did, he saw his adversary clearly—a short, stocky man with a very angry visage.

156

Mickey lurched at Pete, slashing the heavy, wooden oar towards the center of Pete's head.

Pete ducked and the oar slammed into the boathouse wall.

Mickey's right foot flew out from under him. His left foot followed, and Mickey O'Flynn was airborne. A moment later, Pete heard a nauseating thud. Mickey landed squarely on his shoulders. His head snapped backwards. His skull slammed the hardwood deck with a resounding crack. A primeval groan echoed throughout the boathouse. Pete stood crouched waiting for the Irishman to jump to his feet.

But Mickey did not move.

Not a twitch.

Pete grabbed the lantern and shone it into the attacker's face. The man's eyes were open, but his pupils had rolled up into his head. For a moment, Mickey O'Flynn lay teetering in the darkness between life and death. In a dream-world gaze, he turned his head toward Pete and smiled a far-away smile. Slowly, as though he were trying to get to his feet, he leaned over the edge of the boat well toward the abyss of Muscallonge Bay beside him. His knees followed and, at the last moment, Pete grabbed Mickey's coat and pulled him back onto the deck. Pete ran to the *Magpie* and untied the mooring line. He lashed Mickey's feet to his hands, and rolled the lumberjack against the boathouse wall.

Pete stood for a moment, the lantern trained on the unconscious assailant. Blood rushed to Pete's head in pounding torrents. He had to find his friends. *"So quiet and still,"* he remembered. Were they dead or alive?

"Jump aboard. We'll pull the Lyman inside."

CHAPTER 29
RECOVERY

Thursday July 10 10:45 p.m.

Pete grabbed the lantern and flashed it around the boathouse.

"We're going to check out the loft," Pete remembered Dan saying. He shot the lantern's beam into the upper recesses of the seemingly infinite building. There he saw it. A small platform high above the largest of the boat entrances. That's where they are. *"Such good little boys and girls,"* the man had said. *He's killed them*, Pete thought, his emotions turned from relief that he'd survived the assailant's attack to vehement, blind rage. *If that miserable creep killed my friends, he'll wish he drowned.* Pete raced to an area below the platform. He directed the light against the wall and saw a built-in ladder. He scaled it and shined the light along the floor. He saw, in the far corner, three bodies wrapped in blankets bound by yards of anchor line. His heart sank. "Kate!" he screamed, training the light toward the heads of the three motionless bodies. Three pairs of eyes blinked, gazing into Pete's flashlight with profound horror.

Pete stepped from behind the lantern and a muffled gasp of relief exploded from his friends' bound faces. "You're okay!" he shouted. Pete slashed the knots with his knife, first Kate's, then Dan's and Eddie's. In another corner, Pete heard something wiggling against the wall. He flashed the beacon toward it. A shock of blondish-white hair poked through the knotted top of a black, sleeping bag. Pete hurried over and slit the cord. Two hysterical eyes exploded out of the bag.

"Don't kill me!" Neal screamed. He blinked, focussing his eyes. "Pete!" he gasped, looking both grateful and baffled at once. "How'd you get here? What's going on?" He wriggled through the hole and pushed the black bag down from his shoulders. He stood in front of Pete and then looked over at the others as they tore off their bindings. "Where's Mickey?" Neal cried.

"Mickey O'Flynn?" Pete asked. "Was that who jumped me down at the boat? He slipped on the dock and knocked himself cold. I tied him up, but we'd better get down there to make sure he doesn't get loose."

"Where's the other guy?" Neal pressed.

"There's more than one?" Pete asked.

"Yeah!" Neal hollered. "The big guy. Mickey called him `Fats.'"

"Fats?" all four gasped.

"It can't be," Kate whispered. "He was killed two weeks ago in Bosely Channel!"

"That's what Mickey called him," Neal insisted. "Fats."

The others' eyes darted from face to face.

"What else did they say?" Dan probed.

"They said a lot," Neal shouted. "I figured from what Pete told me that this was where the burglar was

159

hiding out. I went into town and bought the biggest lantern Hudson Hardware sells. When it got dark, I rowed over here in the *Magpie* to look around. I no sooner poked the bow under the boathouse door than someone grabbed me. And then a guy said, 'We can't let this kid get away, Mickey.' I heard footsteps come up from behind. Heavy footsteps. The next second, I got whacked on the head and was being zipped into a sleeping bag. Then Mickey said, 'This will work out better than we'd planned, Fats. Go get Pierre. Bring him back here. We'll do away with both of them. We'll fix it to look like Pierre and this kid had a fight and killed each other. We'll leave the empty envelope from that basketball money in Frenchy's coat. By the time the cops find them up there in the loft, we'll be out of the country.'"

"How long ago was that?" Dan asked.

"Maybe an hour ago."

"Then we showed up," Eddie said, shaking his head. "We just waltzed right up the ladder and he picked us off like ducks at a shooting gallery."

"If Neal's right about Fats," Kate said nervously, "we're not out of the woods yet."

"It's Fats, all right," Dan said quickly. "I don't know how he survived the explosion, but he did."

Kate had been staring out the loft window. "Eddie, quick," she said, "turn off the light! A boat's coming along the reed bed." She waited another moment. "It's a canoe. There are two aboard."

"If Fats has Pierre," Dan shouted, "then he's probably got his shotgun, too."

"I've got to get out of here," Neal said, his eyes darting in panic.

"Even if we all could get into Dan's boat," Eddie realized, "we'd never get away from the dock. With Pierre's gun, Fats is close enough right now to blast us out of the water with one shot."

"I've got an idea," Pete said. "Everybody, quick. Get to Dan's boat!"

The five scrambled down the ladder, Pete going first. He shined the light on the last boat well, and they raced to it.

"Jump aboard, Eddie," Pete said. "We'll pull the Lyman inside."

"Pull it inside?" Neal yelled. "That's crazy. Let's blow out of here!"

"Quiet, Neal," Eddie said. "What's your plan, Pete?"

"First," Pete said, "we've got to hide Dan's boat so Fats doesn't know we're here. Then you four surround the dock and wait for Fats to bring his canoe halfway inside. Then you guys grab the bow. I'll swim around from the outside, grab the stern, and together we'll flip him over."

"Wait a minute!" Neal wailed. "Your big idea is to let Fats get inside here with us standing around while you go for a swim? What kind of butt-brained plan is that?"

Dan had ducked his head under the entrance and was looking into the bay. "There he is!" he whispered. "He's coming around the reed bed into the clearing. Fast! Do what Pete says!"

With Dan's boat already mostly inside, Eddie hopped in, grabbed hold of the door, and with one mighty plunge, pulled the big Evinrude underneath. Dan grabbed the bow line and yanked the Lyman inside and out of sight.

As Fats' canoe approached, Pete ran around to the second boat well. He ripped off his shoes and stripped down to his shorts. He slid slowly into the ice-cold water and ducked under the second boathouse door.

The others watched as Pete shoved himself away from the dock. Pete gasped as the frigid water sucked the air from his lungs. He slipped out into the murky blackness of Muscallonge Bay.

Thirty yards to the east two men stroked their way toward Pete. The man in the stern bore the unmistakable bulk of the desperate Mackinac Island dockmaster. He held a double-barreled shotgun across his lap. The bow of the canoe coasted up to the boathouse door.

"Hey, Mickey!" Fats growled inside.

There was no answer as the four teens stood silently around the deck.

"MICKEY!" Fats yelled again.

"Yeah," Eddie answered gruffly, his hand muffling his voice.

"Get ready!" Fats shouted, "I've brought a special guest!"

"Right," Eddie replied.

"Okay, Frenchy," Fats ordered, "lay down in the center of the canoe. We're going in."

Pete opened his eyes. He was inside the Chapman's boathouse.

CHAPTER 30
A TWIST

Thursday, July 10 11:00 p.m.

Pete's plan, to let Fats' canoe get halfway inside before he and his friends leaped into action, seemed like a good idea at the time. But, as for what would happen after that, Pete really hadn't thought that far ahead. Somehow, he figured, the five of them would take care of Fats. They'd whack him on the head, they'd tie him up, or maybe he'd just drown. But the part after that? Well, that was very clear. Pete would swim back into the boathouse, spring up onto the deck, and Kate would leap into his arms. She would fall madly in love with him, and they would live happily ever after. Something like that.

So, as far as the first part not working, that hadn't even entered Pete's mind. Letting Fats' canoe get halfway inside made just enough sense in the moment it flashed through his head that he skipped right over a few major details. Besides, no one else was making any suggestions—except for Neal's moronic idea of just trying to get away. So, now that he'd gotten them

163

to follow his plan, all that was left was to make it work.

As Pete was treading water a few feet out from the boathouse, he recognized his first mistake. He'd forgotten how incredibly cold the Muscallonge Bay water was. Already, he was numb beyond belief. He inhaled deeply as he watched the bow of Fats' canoe slip under the boathouse door.

He calculated exactly how deep he would dive and where he would come up to flip Fats' canoe. He ducked his head under, pushed off against the dock, and propelled himself down and toward Fats. He opened his eyes and discovered a second, and even more critical miscalculation than the first—he was totally blinded by the blackness of the water.

It was like being in his basement at home and his older sister turning off the light from upstairs. Only this was wetter and infinitely colder. Neal's dopey idea was beginning to make a lot more sense. Once under water, Pete had no idea where the canoe was. He was terrified, but he couldn't turn back. This was his idea, and now his friends' lives depended on it—not to mention his own, which, if this didn't work, wouldn't be worth mentioning, anyway.

He scissor-kicked and made several breast strokes underwater. He could tell from the pressure that he was down about six feet; but whether he was near, directly under, or even past his target, he hadn't a clue. Plus, he was out of air. He could easily submarine the entire length of the YMCA pool back home, but that water was heated. Muscallonge Bay, on the other hand, was brutally cold.

A sixth sense, or perhaps wishful thinking, told him that Fats was directly overhead.

Yes, he was sure of it.

He made his move.

Up he charged, kicking with all his might. He reached with both hands for the stern of the canoe. He would push it up and out of the water with one powerful burst of strength. The canoe would turn throwing Fats headlong into the bay.

He exploded from the depths and flew right out of the water, a lot like the trophy bass he'd hooked the week before. This, his third miscalculation, was the worst. He'd missed the canoe by six feet.

He flopped back into the water staring directly into the surprised face of Gerald FitzRoberts. Pete's first wish was that he'd come up six feet closer. His second was that he could be about six miles farther away.

The brilliant moon broke through the clouds cascading a beam of light along the water. Pete's head bobbed at its center. Fats swung the muzzle of his monstrous shotgun in a dead line with Pete's terror-stricken face. Pete gasped and froze, apoplectic in fear. He squeezed his eyes waiting for the blast that would disintegrate his head.

Fats slowly pulled the trigger, a smirk crossing his lips, one eye drawn shut, the other bulging wide down the gun sight. Pete instinctively blinked and jerked his head.

The cannon in Fats' hands exploded just as the stern of the canoe rocketed upwards. A load of buckshot blew off in the general direction of the Big Dipper. The bow of the small craft plunged toward the bottom of the lake.

Inside the boathouse, Eddie crashed his feet again and again onto the front of the canoe. His leaps sent shockwaves along the entire length of the long, narrow craft.

Outside, on the other side of the door, Fats grabbed the canoe gunwales holding himself in the boat. Pierre, who had been lying in the bow, sat up wondering what was happening.

Finally, using his considerable strength, Eddie tipped the boat sideways and Fats exploded from the canoe.

Pete waved his arms as Fats flew toward him. A tremendous splash pushed Pete a few feet away. Still, they remained face to face four feet apart. If Fats reached Pete, he could lock him in his mammoth arms, snap his neck, and send Pete drifting slowly to the depths of Muscallonge Bay.

Fats, however, splashed wildly, his head alternately dropping under water and then popping up, frantically gasping for air.

Could it be that Fats couldn't swim?

Pete hadn't the curiosity to find out. Instead, he spun toward the dock. He reached out with his left arm and took a stroke toward the boathouse kicking ferociously as he did.

From below, however, a mighty hand snatched Pete's right ankle and yanked it down. Pete gulped a breath of air before his head was jerked under. He stroked hard with his hands and arms. He reached the surface, sucked in a breath, and then was immediately pulled back deep into the water. The grip on his leg was excruciating. His lungs screamed in agony.

Nearby, he felt another splash; the concussion sent a torrent of water his way. The approaching wave buoyed Pete's head out of the water. Pete whirled, drew in another breath, and saw, in the moonlight, a mop of blondish-white hair churning the water toward him.

"Pete!" Neal yelled. "Catch!" Neal tossed a large, doughnut-shaped object toward him. The life cushion landed softly in Pete's hands. Pete grabbed it and felt a tug at the other end of the rope.

"Hold on, Pete!" Eddie called out.

Pete clutched the life ring to his chest as Neal bobbed in the water nearby. Pete turned his head but could no longer see Fats who still had a vise-like grip on his leg.

"Keep your head up!" Kate yelled from twenty feet away. "We'll tow you in." It was the voice of an angel.

Eddie had used the lantern to find the pulley rope and raised the boathouse door. Kate stood inside on the dock aiming the lantern out toward Pete.

Fats was slowly drifting downward making it more and more difficult for Pete to keep his head above water. Finally, even the life ring couldn't hold him up on the surface. Pete's ears were exploding as Eddie and Dan strained to drag him toward them.

As the last ounce of air escaped from his lungs, Pete was forced to gasp for another breath. He looked up into a blinding light, his ankle still crushed in Fats' hands.

He inhaled involuntarily just as Dan and Eddie pulled his head out of the water. He drew in air, life.

Pete opened his eyes. He was in the boathouse. Behind him, he heard a loud crack and felt the grip on his leg loosen. Above him, standing on the deck, Pierre LeSoeur grinned as he held a broken paddle in his hands.

Eddie reached into the water and lifted Pete onto the deck.

167

Pierre stood next to Eddie, a broad smile crossing his face. Pierre plunged his arm deep below the surface and snatched a handful of curly, brown hair. He yanked the attached head out of the water and shook it exposing Fats' terrified face to the light. Fats vomited and grabbed for the dock. Pierre shoved him back under water. Finally, using both hands, Pierre hauled Fats onto the deck. While Fats was still heaving uncontrollably, Dan took a length of dock line and bound his legs and hands with every Boy Scout knot in the handbook. Finally, he rolled him against the wall next to Mickey O'Flynn.

Kate shined the light back out of the boathouse and found Neal swimming toward the boarding ladder. Neal pulled himself out of the water shivering and shuddering and looking practically transparent in the moonlight.

"I'm freezing," he cried out.

Kate set the lantern on the floor aiming it toward the rafters. She raced for the loft and, in moments, returned with every blanket and towel she could carry. She passed one each to Eddie and Neal, then threw an extra large blanket around Pete and rubbed his head and back.

"Kate," Eddie said, "take Dan's outboard and go down Bosely to Neal's boathouse. Get Neal's dad on their intercom and ask him to call the sheriff. Tell him we've got the Mackinac Murderer and the man that robbed the basketball money."

Kate jumped in the Lyman, spun it around, and pulled the starter. The Evinrude exploded into action. She shot out of the boathouse across Urie Bay.

An armada of boats made the turn at Connors Point.

CHAPTER 31
THE MACKINAC ARMADA

Thursday July 10 11:20 p.m.

"What time is it?" Neal inquired, keeping his eyes on Fats and Mickey.

"About thirty seconds after the last time you asked," Dan said evenly. "Look, Neal, they'll be here soon. Don't worry."

"It's been ten minutes," Neal said, checking the knots on the hands and legs of the captives. "Kate should be back by now. You don't suppose she ran aground on the way, do you? I've almost done it a hundred times myself."

"I don't think so," Dan replied. "You heard the motor. She checked it down at the end of Urie Bay just like always. She's as good a driver as anyone in the Snows. The moon is bright. It would be like daylight along the channel. Honestly, Neal. She'll be fine."

But Pete was concerned, too. He looked over at Eddie. Eddie glanced at Dan. Dan didn't look all that sure of himself, either.

Pierre glared at Fats and Mickey as if he would just as soon club them both a couple of good ones and save everybody a lot of legal work. Pete stood nearby wondering what could be taking Kate so long. His mind raced through a variety of scenarios, none of which included a favorable outcome. What if Fats or Mickey got loose? The two of them could knock Pierre out and dispatch with the four teenagers quicker than a pike taking a perch.

Fats and Mickey were alert, their eyes darting apprehensively as they sat against the wall. They eyed Pierre nervously as the Frenchman gripped and re-gripped the broken paddle, his vengeful smirk never changing.

"I'm going to look for the electrical panel," Eddie advised the others. "Pete, you and Neal stay here. Dan, bring the lantern. The light switch has to be around somewhere."

As Pete kept a close vigil on Fats and Mickey, Neal stood nearby, towel-drying his hair.

Pete glanced quickly over to Neal. "Nice pass, Neal," Pete said. "I'd have been a goner without you tossing me that life ring when you did."

Neal held the towel at his side and stared evenly at Pete. "Yeah, well, I've got to tell you, when I saw you going after Fats, something in my head snapped. It was like someone turned on a light. You know," Neal said slowly, "you've done something in two weeks that I've tried to do for fifteen years—make the other kids up here be my friends. When I saw you diving in after Fats, I knew why." Neal brushed his head again with the towel. "All this time I was trying to MAKE friends, Pete. What you did was try to BE friends. I've been doing everything I could to impress them with stuff I thought was important; stuff I thought THEY thought was important. So, when I came up here this year, and you had my friends, I hated you for it. That, and I couldn't believe how stupid they were for wanting to be with you instead of me. I had everything. You had nothing. When we had the potluck at your place last night, I looked at you and your cottage and shook my head thinking what a pathetic loser you were. My old play fort out in the woods is bigger than your whole cottage. The motor on my boat probably has more horsepower than your family's car. But YOU had won MY friends. Then I decided I could get along without them. They'd be sorry. What a joke. The other night at the end of the basketball game, I saw you up ahead of me wide open for a lay-up; but I couldn't let you make the last basket to win the game. Instead, I took the long shot. It didn't bother me a bit that I missed and we lost. The important thing was that you didn't make it. And tonight, when they went along with your plan to get Fats, I despised you for that, too."

"That's all right," Pete shrugged. "It worked out. That's all that counts."

"Let me finish, Pete," Neal said, holding up his hand. "Suddenly, I realized that you weren't the loser. It was me. If your plan didn't work, if everyone didn't play as a team, we'd all go down just like in the basketball game—except this wasn't a game. In that flash, I realized that I wanted to be on your side."

Neal stepped toward Pete, his voice wavering. "I'd like to start all over, Pete," Neal said, extending his right hand. "My name is Neal Preston. I'd like to be your friend."

Pete stood speechless, caught completely off guard. For a moment, the two stared at each other, eye to eye. Then a grin worked its way across Pete's face.

"Man, oh, man," he said slowly, "we'll cream those Cedarville guys next year," and he raised his right hand to return Neal's grip.

Dan and Eddie came back from their unsuccessful search for the light panel. A faint hum of a distant boat engine broke the silence.

"Over there," Dan yelled, pointing through the boathouse entrance. "Someone's coming."

The white running light of a single boat made the turn from Connors Point to a straight line towards them. All else was quiet as they watched the approaching vessel.

Gradually, a low, rumbling thunder grew in the distance. It seemed to come from all directions at once.

"What is that?" Pete asked.

"I don't know," Neal answered. "It sounds like a squadron of B-52's. We're not at war with Canada, are we?"

"I don't think so," Dan grinned. "At least, there's been nothing about it in the Weekly Wave."

Following the first boat by about a hundred yards, a second light appeared. Then, a steady stream of white points flowed into Elliot Bay. Pete looked down Snows Channel toward Hessel. He glanced over into Urie Bay. Running lights filled the horizon.

Somehow Kate had gotten word out to, what seemed to be, the entire population of Mackinac County. They had mobilized and were charging into battle like the six hundred soldiers of the Light Brigade. Thunder swelled as boats poured in from every point on the compass.

Soon, pleasure craft of all sizes sat in front of Chapman's boathouse with their flashlights, lanterns, and search beams trained on the small entrance. Muscallonge Bay practically throbbed with boat engines purring in neutral.

The first to arrive, Con Shoberg's thirty-foot-long police boat, moved in cautiously. The sheriff stood in the bow, his handgun drawn. He peered in with his flashlight directed into the small portal. "Well, it looks like you don't need me," he laughed holstering his gun. "I'd say you've got things pretty well in control. Who are these men?"

"This is Gerald FitzRoberts," Dan said. "He killed the man on Mackinac Island and nearly killed us."

"And this is Mickey O'Flynn," Kate added. "He attacked the doctor and stole the money after the basketball game."

"And here's the money, Sheriff," Eddie said, handing Mr. Shoberg the envelope. "We found it up in the loft."

"Well, I'll be," Sheriff Shoberg exclaimed. "I guess the Hessel boy will get his iron lung after all."

From the back of the fleet came another boat. The *Silver Moon* coasted in with the Terkels, Hinkens, and Jenkins peering anxiously ahead. Smiles of relief broke out at the discovery that everyone was safe.

Dr. Hinken stepped to the bow. "I hope you kids have cleaned up all the crime around here," he smiled. "I'd like to remind you that some of us came north to relax.

"I believe they have," Sheriff Shoberg said. "But if anything does come up, you can bet I'm not letting them in on it. It's hard enough getting elected around here without a bunch of teenagers showing me up all the time."

The sheriff stepped onto the dock. In the shadows, he saw a man holding a broken paddle. "Hey, what's this?" he asked, reaching for his gun.

"That's Pierre LeSoeur," Eddie answered quickly. "He helped us flip the canoe and capture Fats."

"Well, I guess I had you pegged wrong all the time, Pierre," Sheriff Shoberg said. "I sure could use your help right now bringing these two prisoners into town. How'd you like to be my deputy?"

"<u>Mais oui, monsieur,</u> I would like that very much," Pierre replied, raising the paddle.

The sheriff handed Pierre two pairs of handcuffs. The Frenchman snapped a set each on Fats' and Mickey's wrists and shoved them into the back of the police boat. Con Shoberg turned and faced the flotilla around him. "All right, everybody, the party's over. Let's go home."

He started the engine and backed away from the boathouse. The motor roared and the police boat thundered across Muscallonge Bay toward Cedarville. One by one, the hundred or so other boats turned away leaving only the *Silver Moon* with all the parents and the red and white Lyman with Kate sitting in the stern. The four boys stood together within the boathouse, the lantern still shining on them.

"I thought you might want to know," Mr. Terkel said, breaking the silence, "I've taken Harold Geetings' case as his legal counsel. The trial begins tomorrow in St. Ignace. We'll probably need to stay the rest of the summer rather than return next week to Cincinnati as we'd planned. Maybe you would like to take the *Griffin* back to Mackinac sometime. You could visit with the Andersons for a few days and show Pete what the Island's really like. What do you think of that?"

"Are you kidding?" Eddie said. "That would be great! What about Dan and Kate? Are the Hinkens staying, too?"

"Yes," Dr. Hinken said. "Harold will need us as character witnesses. Each of you will have to take the stand for what you saw and heard both here and on Mackinac. Your testimony will be the most important part of his defense."

"We'll all be part of it," Pete's mom added. "Harold built such a wall around himself over the years that he not only lived on an island, he became one as well. It wasn't until that moment in Bosely Channel when he and Fats were chasing you that he realized how important friends are. The wall he had built suddenly crumbled. He knew he had to protect you even though it would send him to jail, perhaps for the rest of his life."

Neal stepped forward. "I got up here too late this summer to be in on the Geetings affair," Neal said thoughtfully, "but it sounds like he and I had a lot in common. Both of us had great friends all around us but neither were willing to accept their friendship. I know what he must have felt when he saved you guys in Bosely Channel," Neal said, looking at his friends. "I felt the same thing when Pete and Fats were fighting outside the boathouse and Fats kept pulling Pete's head under water. I looked around and saw the ring buoy hanging on the wall. In that moment, the weight of a mountain fell from my shoulders. I handed the end of the rope to Eddie and, I swear, I could have _walked_ the life preserver out to Pete. And I would have, too, but I was afraid people might think I was showing off," Neal smiled, tears of joy streaming down his face.

175

"Oh, Neal," Kate laughed. "You don't know how good this feels. You've been such a load. We tried everything to make you realize what you were doing. I guess you had to see it for yourself."

"Let's head home," Pete said. "I'm tired. I've been saved twice now, once by Harold Geetings in Bosely Channel and now here, by Neal. How about we get some sleep."

Dan, Eddie, and Pete joined Kate in the red and white Lyman as the *Silver Moon* turned and headed for Elliot Bay. Dan started the Evinrude and idled her down to shifting range. Pete nudged Dan and nodded over to Neal who was still standing next to the *Magpie*.

"Are you going to be able to get home, Neal?" Pete asked.

"I don't know," Neal replied. "It looks as if I'm down to one oar. Do you suppose you could give me a tow?"

"You bet, Neal," Pete said, grabbing the Lyman's anchor rope. "I guess it's my turn to throw you a lifeline. Hop in the *Magpie* and hold tight. We'll have you home in no time."